Antti Tuuri

The Winter War

Antti Tuuri

Acknowledgements

Aspasia Books, Inc. wishes to thank
the Finnish Literature Information Centre for its generous translation support
and FINNKINO Oy for the rights to use two photographs from
Pekka Parikka's film *Talvisota* (1988)

ASPASIA CLASSICS IN FINNISH LITERATURE

Antti Tuuri

The Winter War

Translated by
Richard Impola

Aspasia Books
Beaverton, Ontario, Canada

The Winter War
ISBN 0-9731053-7-2 (bound); ISBN 0-9731053-3-X (pbk.)
ISSN 1498-8348

Published in 2003 by Aspasia Books, Inc.
B25040 Maple Beach Road, R.R.1, Beaverton, Ontario, L0K 1A0, Canada
aspasia@aspasiabooks.com
www.aspasiabooks.com

Translated from the Finnish *Talvisota*
First published in Finland by Otava (Helsinki, Finland)
Copyright © 1984 Antti Tuuri (Finnish original)
Copyright © 2003 Richard Impola (English translation)
Copyright © 2003 Aspasia Books, Inc. (English language edition)

Cover design by Martin Best of My6productions.com

Photographs on front and back cover courtesy of Finnkino Oy.

*Aspasia Books gratefully acknowledges the generous assistance of the
Finnish Literature Information Center.*

Introduction by Börje Vähämäki
Aspasia Classics in Finnish Literature series editor: Börje Vähämäki

* * * * * *

National Library of Canada Cataloguing in Publication

Tuuri, Antti, 1944-
    The winter war / Antti Tuuri ; translated by Richard Impola.

(Aspasia classics in Finnish literature, ISSN 1498-8348)
Translation of: Talvisota, first published in Finnish in 1984.
ISBN 0-9731053-7-2 (bound).--ISBN 0-9731053-3-X (pbk.)

    1. Russo-Finnish War, 1939-1940--Fiction. I. Impola, Richard, 1923-
II. Title. III. Series.

PH355.T82T3413 2003   894'.54133   C2003-906925-7

INTRODUCTION

Since the Declaration of Independence on December 6, 1917, Finland has experienced four wars: The Civil War (1918), The Winter War (1939–1940), The Continuation War (1941–1944), and the German or Lapland War (1944–45) The Civil War still captures many writers' and scholars' imagination, yet Väinö Linna's account in *Under the North Star 2: The Uprising* (original 1960, English translation 2002) is still considered the best literary treatment of that tragic episode in Finland's history. Similarly, The Continuation War is superbly described in Väinö Linna's *The Unknown Soldier* (1954, English 1957). In contrast, the Lapland (German) War has received little attention by Finland's authors. The Winter War is the war Finns continue to remember as the "good" or the "heroic" war. Surprisingly, the Winter War did not have a definitive novel to its name before Antti Tuuri in 1984 published *Talvisota*, a book that now lies before us in English translation. A literary classic dealing with the Winter War — and actually mentioned by Hakala in Tuuri's *The Winter War* — is a poetry collection entitled *Kiirastuli* (1940) "Fires of Purgatory" by Yrjö Jylhä, who was a company commander at Kirvesmäki.

The Winter War began dramatically with the Soviet Union's

air attack on Helsinki in the morning of November 30, 1939 and ended on March 13, 1940. As a buffer zone, the Soviet Union had demanded a good portion of Karelia, particularly the Karelian Isthmus, referred to by Finns simply as *Kannas*, for the protection of Leningrad. They also demanded a naval base in the Hanko region in south western Finland, as well as Finland's only Arctic Sea port, Petsamo. Finland refused to acquiesce, however, and while continuing negotiations made preparations in anticipation of a possible attack by the Soviet Union.

The Winter War soon caught the attention of the Western world, which predicted Finland would last a week, or ten days at best. The overwhelmingly superior strength in men and armaments seemed to make the Soviet Union too formidable an enemy. To most nations' surprise, the Finns stubbornly held the Russians at bay, even recorded several victories as the headlines in North American newspapers declared in large letters: "FINNS SMASH INVADERS ON FOUR FRONTS, ANNIHILATE FLOWER OF RUSSIAN ARMY or 60 RUSS PLANES REPORTED DESTROYED IN FINNISH BOMB ATTACK ON MURMANSK, SOVIET DRIVEN BACK WITH HEAVY LOSS." The Winter War lasted 105 days in record cold conditions with heavy losses on both sides. Finland lost almost 23,000 men with over 43,000 wounded while the Russians are reported to have sustained losses of more than 125,000 dead and 265,000 wounded. The Russian dominance in numbers finally became overwhelming and the Finns were forced to accept peace terms very similar to the original Soviet demands: secession of the Karelian Isthmus with the old Finnish city of Vyborg, where some 12% of Finland's population lived, the Petsamo harbor, and Hanko. About 450,000 Karelians were evacuated to Finland.

The military leadership of independent Finland came from two different backgrounds: those trained in the Czarist military, including Marshal Mannerheim, and those trained as Jaegers in Germany during WWI. After the Civil War of 1918, in which "the Reds" rebelled, but lost to "the Whites", the Civil Guard was reconstituted as a (White) reserve guard. These terms are used in the novel.

Antti Tuuri writes terse, succinct prose in his tradition of objective prose. This is true despite the fact that the entire novel is written as told by one man, Martti Hakala. Hakala tells the story of the war as he experienced it, from his personal location, making it clear how little or how much the ordinary soldier knew about the larger war picture and how sometimes contradictory rumors circulated. The language, consequently, sports features of spoken language, although the narrator most often stays within the norm of standard Finnish. Tuuri does, however, give Hakala a personal style of speech and a matter-of-fact style and tone of voice. His rich humor is quiet and understated. The spoken language is reflected in expressions commonly used in Finnish conversations, such as frequent use of the phrase "our neighbor" when referring to Russians; in Finnish vernacular in the post-war years the terms "our neighbor" and "our enemy" were interchangeable.

Martti Hakala is of the same Hakala family Tuuri depicts in his so-called Ostrobothnia suite. The popular series includes six novels: *Pohjanmaa* (1982), published in English by Aspasia Books as *A Day in Ostrobothnia* (2001) in translation by Anselm Hollo, *Talvisota* (1984) in English by Aspasia Books, Inc. as *The Winter War* (2003) in translation by Richard Impola, *Ameriikan Raitti* "Paradise America" (1986), *Uusi Jerusalem*

"New Jerusalem" (1988), *Maan avaruus* "Earth's Vastness"(1989). The latest installment in the Ostrobothnia series is *Lakeuden kutsu* "The Call of the Plains" (1997), which earned Antti Tuuri the prestigious Finlandia Prize for Finnish Literature.

Martti Hakala was a member of the 23rd Infantry regiment which was made up almost entirely of men from the province of Ostrobothnia in central western Finland. In such regionally composed battalions, regiments, and companies men were more closely knit, often knew each other, or of each other, and perhaps felt a need to uphold certain local reputations. The stereotypical image of Ostrobothnians emphasizes their courage, patriotism, seriousness, their love of freedom, their independent spirit, and their proneness to bravado that borders on wildness.

The novel is littered with references to Ostrobothnian communities and phenomena, most of which involve South Ostrobothnia. For example, the reference to revivalist meetings reflects the strength of religious revivalism in Ostrobothnia. Ostrobothnian towns mentioned include Seinäjoki, Lapua, Ylihärmä, Soini, Lehtimäki, Ylistaro, Kuortane, Jalasjärvi, Jurva, Isokyrö and Laihia. Some towns have more distinct reputations than others and Tuuri allows those reputations to play out in the novel. Thus, for example, Laihia is stereotyped with extreme thrift or stinginess, Jurva is known still today for its wood carvers and furniture makers, and Härmä evokes connotations of aggressive behavior, "tough guys", and loud singing, a reputation that was further cemented in such novels as Santeri Alkio's *Puukkojunkkarit* "The Ruffians with the Knives" (1894) and Artturi Järviluoma's play *Pohjalaisia* "Ostrobothnians" (1914).

Most of the Ostrobothnian towns mentioned in Tuuri's novel are landlocked, because the coastal towns on Finland's western shore are largely Swedish-speaking, having been settled many centuries ago from Sweden across the Gulf of Bothnia. The Swedish-speakers are a reminder of the Swedish era (1157-1809) when Finland was the eastern province of Sweden. The Swedish-speakers in coastal Ostrobothnia are Finns, but many do not speak Finnish. There were, however, also Swedish volunteers from Sweden in The Winter War. The Swedish volunteers are called Swedes while the Swedish-speaking Finns are called Finland-Swedes.

About 8000 volunteers from Sweden, 700-800 from Norway and Denmark each, as well as Estonian and Hungarian volunteers, fought for Finland in the war. Psychologically important were the 400 American and Canadian Finns who volunteered in the Winter War. Many more were actually in training or ready to make the journey to Finland when peace was announced.

The events in The Winter War novel are played out in a relatively small area on the eastern side of the Isthmus of Karelia, near Lake Ladoga: Taipale River and later Vuosalmi. The home front firmly believed Finland was doing well in the war, and the international press continued to focus on Finland's successes to the very end of the war. The announcement of peace, therefore, came abruptly and as a surprise. Many of Finland's soldiers were dejected when they learned about the harsh conditions of the armistice. They had thought the Finns were winning the war or at least holding their own.

Börje Vähämäki

The Winter War

A Narrative

I

I said let's walk, it isn't far to the school. But my brother said no, we don't go off to war from our house on foot. So we hitched up the horse and Jussi went along to drive. His card hadn't come yet — he was still too young for this war.

We had to be at the school by nine so we set off early in the evening with Socks pulling the buggy. The village street was crowded with men walking or driving horses or riding bicycles. Many had an escort. Almost everyone looked serious. No one knew what to expect or what this call-up for refresher training was all about.

There were four hundred of us gathered at the school. Almost every man in the parish was there. I knew most of them, especially the men from the neighboring village and from the church village. Others I knew less well — from revivalist meetings and county affairs or from my confirmation class. And of course there were the men from my own village.

Even in one parish, you get all kinds. Two brothers had quarreled over a bottle of whiskey. They must have had a drink or two along the way. One brought a bottle of vodka with him into the schoolyard, but the others drank it, not exactly in secret but cunningly. They all got into a fight over it. Several of us had to pull them apart and hang onto them to keep them from killing each other before the war had even begun. My brother Paavo said the Russians were in for a hard time with us, since the men could hardly be held back even when just starting out.

One man sat in the middle of the floor and ate oven-baked pancake from his pack, so old it had turned almost blue. I didn't know him. His pack was an old fertilizer sack with rocks in the corners, where he had tied ropes for shoulder straps. When I asked the boys who he was, they told me he was going to be our company cook, that he would make our meals in the war. Altogether different men cooked for us on The Isthmus of Karelia, which became so famous all Finns refer to it in Finnish simply as *Kannas*. It was a joke, he never became our cook. I never saw the man after we left Seinäjoki, they must have sent him back home. But later I often thought our cooks were little better than the man sitting on the floor of the schoolhouse eating his rancid oven pancake.

At nine we were ordered into four columns and we obeyed. Equipment — what there was of it — had been issued during the evening. It was the thirteenth of October. The district commander of the Civil Guard, who was to become our company commander, gave a speech and then marched us to the railroad station. The roadsides were lined with women and children who followed us to the station. Many people were already there waiting.

We waited for the train to leave, saying goodbye to those who were staying at home. Of course it was much easier for unmarried, men without ties. But I had a wife and a son seeing me off. One didn't think of anything funny to say. It was not fun. We talked about home and practical matters — at least we'd finished the fall chores so that the women weren't left with them unfinished.

Our Paavo was a bachelor, but he too had some girl hanging on his lapels, sobbing away. He'd said nothing about her at home, and as we jolted along toward Seinäjoki in the cattle car, the other bachelors teased him about it: they asked if she'd gotten close enough to the cattle cars and the bulls to get a whiff of them. I think Paavo must really have been in love with the girl because he didn't start wagging his tongue about her to the boys. He sat silent at the door of the cattle car and watched the landscape and the lights of the houses and the stations flashing by. Every time I've seen that girl since then, I've thought of how serious my kid brother had been all the way to Seinäjoki. He was usually so cheerful. The girl is now Jussi Rinta's wife. I've never talked to her about what she and Paavo may have had in mind.

Leaving was sure sad for many, but sorrow doesn't last for long in a gang like that. Some had a liquor bottle at the bottom of their packs, and the boys sampled a bit of it. Then they whooped out a few war songs to raise their spirits. The trip to Seinäjoki lasted the whole night, and we couldn't really sleep since after all we were going toward an unknown destination — all autumn long we'd been reading about the negotiations our government was carrying on in Moscow, about the Russian demands for a piece of Finland. They had so little land at home that they needed more.

In our opinion the Russians had all the land they needed. We figured that if it came to a crunch, we could maybe give them the one by two meter plot a man needs for a grave.

II

We had to wait for a week in Seinäjoki, and we didn't know for sure if we'd have to go anywhere. They gave us more equipment there, along with rifles for those who had none. Those of us who belonged to the Civil Guard had our own weapons. It turned out that those guns were getting to be in poor shape, the rifling in the barrels worn from firing. But the army-issue rifles were in good shape; they came straight from a supply-room, many of them brand-new. We looked them over and figured you could hit with them, especially if you happened to squeeze the trigger just when the bead hit the target. But the men who got the new weapons here, those who weren't in the Guard, had never done much shooting. They gave us nastier weapons too, machine pistols and automatic rifles, but no ammunition for fear of accidents.

There's been a lot of talk about the equipment the men had for the Winter War. You have to admit it was bad. Many got nothing from the Army but a cockade for their hats and an army belt to buckle around their coats. They went through the whole war in their own clothes; the only way to know a soldier in the Finnish army was by his cockade or army belt. As late as March at Vuosalmi I saw one of the boys from our parish still wearing the blue suede-cloth blouse he'd worn when he went off to war. He came home in it too, although by way of an army hospital, his legs full of shrapnel. They patched him up. But the suede-cloth blouse came through whole.

Infantry Regiment 23 was put together at Seinäjoki and was made up almost entirely of men from Ostrobothnia. Its commanding officer was Lieutenant Colonel Matti Laurila. We were in the regiment's second battalion. All the while we were in Seinäjoki, we were quartered in the Jouppi house in Jouppila village.

It was total confusion in Seinäjoki. Everyone tried to grab as much as he could for himself in case we had to go off to war. The plans were clear enough and the allotments precise: the goods were to be distributed so that everyone got his share. But everything went wrong from the start. For instance, we came close to going without a field kitchen. We did get word we would get one, but that word didn't do us much good. Our field kitchen was nowhere to be found, although all of us actually went searching the town for it. We decided that a kitchen was crucial in war and swore we wouldn't leave Seinäjoki without one. A lotta from the women's auxiliary in town told us she had seen a tarp-covered field kitchen in a schoolyard, so our boys went to get it. We just took it for our company. Nobody came around to ask about it. It turned out to be a vital piece of equipment during the whole war and cooked many a batch of oatmeal there on *The Isthmus*.

When they started splitting the men up into squads, Paavo and I went and asked the platoon leader to put us in the same squad so we could help each other in tight places. I said I could sort of look after Paavo: he was so young and inexperienced and needed someone to take care of him. They did put us in the same squad, but that didn't help much in the places they sent us to. I didn't do very well at protecting or taking care of him.

Maybe it was out of deviltry that they put Erkkilä in our squad after Paavo and I went to talk to them about how brothers could help each other in war. People said Erkkilä was the son of our father and a maidservant he had paid off. His mother, Maija Erkkilä, had in fact worked for us, but had left before the child was born. We never mentioned it at home, but there was talk in the village. After Father left for America, we said very little about him. I understood Mother well. She didn't want to talk about such things to her sons, religious, hard-working woman that she was. I was the same age as Erkkilä and had been his confirmation-school classmate, although we never spent much time together. We had known each other since childhood, but we both shied away from contacts because of the village talk.

So they put Erkkilä into our squad. It was at full strength when we left Seinäjoki, seven men and a squad leader. I was the only one who came out alive. Those who survived the Winter War died in the Continuation War. It was no good-luck squad they put together at Seinäjoki. But we didn't know it at the time.

III

They began teaching us at Seinäjoki, close-order drills with rifles and other skills necessary in this business of war. We had to repeat old routines we'd learned in the army. We were all humble and obedient then. The times were like that.

The officers gave us lectures on the world political situation and what Russia had in mind for us, and what had happened to the Estonians and the other countries south of the Baltic Sea because they had believed what the Russians had said and had given them lands and military bases. We all came to the conclusion that we shouldn't give in to our oppressors and that if they couldn't trust us never to attack Leningrad unless we gave them the Hanko peninsula and part of *The Isthmus*, so what? We didn't trust them very much either.

We could have gone home any number of times to get more food and gear if we had known when we first came that we would be spending weeks in Seinäjoki. But we didn't known it then. We kept chasing after supplies and battling with the logistics troops for every little thing we needed. It was a full-time job holding our own against them and the other outfits and coping with the regular army training program to boot.

They put together nine infantry companies at Seinäjoki: from

Ylistaro, Ylihärmä, Kuortane, Töysä, Lapua, Jalasjärvi, Jurva, Isokyrö, from almost everywhere around Ostrobothnia. In the regimental column there were infantry and machine-gun companies, headquarters men, signal corps, and horsemen from Lapua. This is what we had to contend with.

Whenever we had time off from getting supplies and other duties, we looked around Seinäjoki. There wasn't much to look at then or even later. It was a market town that had shot up at the crossing of the Vaasa and Ostrobothnia railroads: low wooden houses, and always horseshit on the streets.

The tough thing for a soldier, when he is waiting for a war and during one, is that he is never told anything. All he can do is sit and wait until someone comes along and gives him an order. Then he has to do what he's told. Those in command of our regiment must have known well in advance when and how we would be sent on from Seinäjoki, for trains had to be reserved many days before we were shipped, but they told us nothing. We were kept completely in the dark. That gave rise to all kinds of rumors, for in any group of men there is always someone who pretends to know, and his stories spread quickly, getting better and better along the way. And many believed the stories, at least at first.

In our company the story was told as absolute truth that the Russians would not dare to attack Finland because the Swedes had given our government a guarantee that they would come to our aid at once if Russia attacked. Many believed the rumor. I didn't. The Russians were not the least bit afraid of the Swedes, I thought.

On the eighteenth of October we finally left Seinäjoki. They still didn't tell us exactly where we were going. Our whole second battalion was on the same train and other battalions had their own trains. It was Sunday when we left. Only at the Haapamäki station did we see that we were headed east, for there the train turned onto the Jyväskylä track. They said that it was only in Haapamäki that our battalion commander, Captain Järvinen, was handed an envelope with written orders about where we were going and how.

Not until the following day did the battalion get off the train. We saw that we were at the Inkilä station. We were on the Karelian Isthmus. We sure had come far from our home parish. Many of us had never been so far from home, not even I, nor Paavo. It had been quite a trip. The load was so heavy that a part of the train even broke loose on the way — a whole battalion of men with its horses and equipment. The locomotive crew did not even notice, but drove on for kilometers before they got word that the tail end of the train was missing, along with a lot of men who were bound for the war. So the crew backed the train up to where its tail end was sitting on the rails. That happened in the village of Kintaus. I never did find out where this village of Kintaus was or is — we'd had to jolt along in the cattle cars for a long time before we got to Inkilä.

We tried to kill time on the train in many ways. I seem to remember that we laughed a lot as we sat in the cars on our way to war through Finland. We had no idea what war was like. I don't remember now what kind of stories we laughed at. Right after the war, I sometimes tried to tell them to people at home, but they didn't think them at all funny. So then I forgot them too.

When you're traveling with a bunch of men like that — young men — some wisecracker or storyteller always pops up who needs only to say a couple of words or make a face to start the whole gang laughing fit to bust. You can't repeat these stories to others, they're too much a part of a situation. The stories told on the train were tied in with the fact that we were being taken toward an unknown place and an unknown fate, and we knew that if war came, it was likely that many of us would never get to sit jolting on a train on the way back to our home parish. So we laughed at almost anything.

Sometimes the older men got tired of the laughing and started to order us around in the cattle car, but often they too were in a mood to talk. Everyone felt loose. The officers were traveling in their own coaches and the men were free of them the whole way; our car had only privates and non-coms. A cattle car is no comfortable sleeper, but it did not demand much of us. We tried to sleep, made coffee on the stove, kept the stove and the car warm with birch wood, and then there were those story sessions. We always got a big kick out of it when someone had to relieve himself out the door of the car. That was the kind of fun we had.

IV

At the Inkilä station we unloaded the train as if enemy planes were over us the whole time, harrying us with an air attack. It was the army's way of trying at every turn to teach us what real war would be like. We ran around with packs on our backs and guns in hand, dragging the goods from the cattle car into the woods in back of the station. There we assembled, sheltered from air attack by the trees. It was about four o'clock in the afternoon.

The boys brought the horses and their wagons from the train and hitched them up under cover of the woods. We loaded the wagons there too. The officers from the regimental level on down to company commanders had horses to ride. The platoon leaders had none. The plans for waging the war, based on experience gained in the War of Independence, was for the officers to dash on horseback from one unit to another, giving orders to the men and raising their morale. Those horses were of no use at Taipale or Vuosalmi. They all wound up hauling freight.

The older men, who had been in the War of Independence, built fires and started to make coffee. They said it would take a long time for a battalion of men and their gear to get moving, that we were in no hurry. Our squad leader was horrified — the enemy could see the smoke from their fires and send pursuit planes to strafe us and fleets of bombers to attack us. But his talk didn't faze the older men. They said the war would begin only when the Russian machine guns started to sing. They felt like having coffee so they made some. The rest of us didn't dare. One of the older men said he'd been there when Tampere was taken in 1918 and had gone on the expeditions to Estonia and Aunus. They had lost lots of boys in all those places. He said he'd seen a lot more there than the South Ostrobothnia District Guard passing in review at Seinäjoki. He said the squad leaders would have more cause to turn pale when the machine guns started to sing than at the lighting of a campfire or two in the woods back of the Inkilä station.

The boys got the goods unloaded from the train, although they weren't sheltered from air attacks during the entire unloading. The third battalion's train had already stopped at the station to wait for unloading when we got there. Although the boys on board were supposed to wait for the order to begin unloading, they refused to sit in the cattle cars for long. They went to look around in back of the station and along the tracks in the railroad yard. Their officers were in the very first coach from where they had a hard time keeping watch on them. When they noticed that half the battalion was strolling around the station yard, they rushed out to jerk the boys to attention, form them up, and march them back into the cattle cars so that the unloading could proceed as originally planned, under cover from air attack. The first battalion's train had already been unloaded when we came into the station and its boys were already marching along the highway when we began running across the station yard into the shelter of the woods.

The march command was given and we started out. The battalion's companies marched in numerical order, their officers mounted on horses, except for our company commander. He never rode, but ordered those of us he knew to take turns on his horse. So we all got to ride on the commander's horse during the night the march lasted, almost everyone in the company. I rode a little while too, thinking that a horse's back wasn't a very safe place in a modern war, that one of our neighbor's riflemen might drop a rider from it like a grouse from a tree. My brother rode the horse too, shouting for someone to bring him an officer's sword now, so he could practice mowing down Russians with it. He was only twenty years old then, my brother.

Twilight fell almost as soon as we began to march, and before long it was pitch dark. Lights that would reveal troop movements to the enemy were forbidden. But the road always loomed ahead of us as a pale streak, and along that pale streak we marched toward openings in the woods on the crests of hills. There were lots of hills on the way from Inkilä to Räisälä, and the harnesses on our horses were just not made for that kind of terrain. Our other horse gear was in miserable condition too. All the horses had been requisitioned, along with their equipment. Everyone had tried to palm off his poorest old stuff on the army.

We had real trouble with the harnesses. There were no hill bands for the horses — the harnesses were made for level ground — the horses could not pull loads uphill with them, nor could they brake on the way down. They had only the breeching to depend on. The men had to hang on to the wagons on the down-hill and push them on the uphill. And there were lots of hills.

After the war when the evacuees from Karelia drove horses with hill bands through our counties, the people laughed, especially the women. But those of us who remembered the hills on the road from Inkilä to Räisälä didn't feel at all like laughing. The

Karelians had their own name for the hill bands, but I don't remember it. The bands were kind of broad, with adornments. Our horses had only breechings to bear the whole weight of the load on the downhills, and they ripped open the hindquarters of the horses.

Many of the boys on the way to war had bought themselves new leather boots, which rubbed their feet raw after a few hours of marching. Their joking changed to cursing. On the first night, half the company had god-awful blisters on their feet. I had worn my old boots when I left home, thinking the army would give us new ones. It was my good luck that they had none. My feet stayed whole. With those boots I tramped the bosom of my fatherland for many years, and they never rubbed at all.

We marched the whole evening and far into the night, tugging at the horses and their loads uphill and down. After midnight we came to a village where housing had been arranged for us. I never found out the name of the place. Our whole company was put into one house to sleep. The people of the house were still there. They put us into the main room, to sleep on the floor. Men were lying on benches, on tables, and under tables. Some of them had to go into outbuildings. The officers slept in the bedroom with the owner of the house and his wife. The children slept with us in the main room.

I woke up in the wee hours of the morning from a dream. I thought I was suffocating. I had fallen into the clay pit in back of our house, was lying at the bottom of it, looking at the algae and slime and pollywogs swimming there, so many that the bottom of the pit was almost black. In my dream I knew I mustn't breathe under the water, I would get water into my lungs and drown. But it was hard to hold my breath, and my chest hurt. I knew

I wouldn't be able to hold my breath forever and would have to give in. Before I woke up I wondered that breathing water was no different from breathing air, only somewhat sweeter, as if the air had been sprayed with some sweet-smelling gas.

When I woke up, I rose and tried to get out by fitting my feet between the boys sleeping on the floor. But they were so close together there wasn't room for my feet. I had to walk over them. Many were so tired from marching they did not stir even when I had to step with my whole weight on them. In the dark room I couldn't even tell what part of the body I was stepping on.

Out in the yard I sat on the steps and took deep breaths of the fresh air. It was a cold night. The man on guard duty came to chat with me. Time was passing slowly for him since he had no watch, and he asked me what time it was. I told him it was about five in the morning. Soon after that, someone shouted a wake-up call. The boys in the main room woke up and the officers came from the back bedroom. The children chatted with us, asked when we would leave. They were not at all polite, their parents, husband and wife, tried to hush them.

For breakfast we had tea and biscuits. With that nourishment we had to set out marching. The day dawned, but marching wasn't easy today either, for the road was again uphill and down all the way. There didn't seem to be a single level stretch, and those hills were no hillocks either. Out our way every one of them would have been called a mountain.

We had been told we were marching toward Unnunkoski in the parish of Räisälä, to start waiting for war in earnest. Or for peace. We couldn't think of that now, marching and moving forward were first and foremost in our minds. We were even ordered to sing, but not much came of it. The men from Ylihärmä were marching behind us, and they sang their own songs first, and then the newer war songs. Our officers tried urging us to sing so that the Ylihärmä company wouldn't get the reputation of being the battalion's best singers, but we didn't care about that honor. We vowed to pursue another kind of honor, a more warlike one, if we got the chance; the honor for singing we'd leave entirely to the men of Ylihärmä. They were marching right behind us so we could hear their singing very well, especially Kalle Takala. We could clearly hear him above the rest. They sang, "You can stay with Hessa, I'll lie down with Liisa," over and over. They must have sung many other songs that day, but none of them stuck in my mind. And as the day wore on and we didn't catch sight of Unnunkoski ahead of us, even the Härmä singers slacked off.

It seemed incomprehensible that we had no idea how far we had to go and how long we had to stay. During Civil Guard training we had always known that our troubles would soon be over and that we would get home. You can put up with lots of trials and troubles, rubbing boots and heavy loads, when you know for sure they will come to an end. But on this march to Unnunkoski we began to understand something about going to war: The future didn't give us any certainty that we could cling to and organize our lives around. In fact, we didn't have any future. That felt bad, and put many of us in a foul mood. By early afternoon some of us were saying that if the men from Ylihärmä didn't quit that braying we would stop and shut their mouths with a knuckle sandwich. Later in the afternoon we all felt like that.

V

We reached Unnunkoski only in late afternoon. We were all so tired from marching and lack of sleep the day before that we fell asleep right away. Tents had been pitched and heated for us and we slept in them the first night. A fire watch and guard duty were posted and the rest of us got to sleep.

At five in the morning a monstrous trumpet blast woke us up. No one could imagine what it was — was it the doomsday trumpet, along with all that neighing of horses and shouting? We snatched up our guns and charged out of the tents, sure that war had come to Unnunkoski. We'd had no chance to check out the place the day before. A river ran through the village and now there was a steamboat on the river. The crew had started heating the steam boilers in the morning and when the pressure was high enough they blew the boat's whistle. It was their signal to the villagers that the boat was leaving for Käkisalmi. Many of us had never seen a ship before, and fewer yet had seen this marvel — a ship that could sail on a river. Our horses were not used to the sound of the ship's steam whistle. It spooked them into running through the village streets, around the fields, and into the woods beyond. Our drivers were running after them, trying to calm them down, many with pack on back and rifle in hand, thinking the war had broken out and the Russians were attacking us while we slept. It took them a long time to catch the horses.

We started off down the river bank. The dock was full of Karelians: almost the whole village was there loading the boat. It carried milk from Unnunkoski to the cooperative dairy in Käkisalmi, and its crew took care of villagers' business there; the villagers were gathered on the dock to make the arrangements. There was a lot of talk and outbursts of laughter; you know how those Karelians are.

The village men had all been taken to the border to work on fortifications and to wait in case the Russians attacked. That's what they told us. There was not a single man fit for war left in the village, only women, children, and old men. So many of us from Ostrobothnia gathered around that soon there were many companies on the river bank and the dock.

They told us that the river was the Vuoksi, or one branch of the Vuoksi. It has many branches that flow into Lake Ladoga. This village of Vuoksi was on the banks of one of those branches. The Taipale River was another of those branches; its waters hook toward Suvanto and also flow into Ladoga. Later we got to see a lot of that river.

The river flowing through Unnunkoski was not very wide, but it must have been deep for a steamboat to sail on it. We made jokes about the Karelians having a different kind of milk truck than in the rest of the country.

Some of the boys had already got to talking with the Karelian women before we were ordered back to camp. When the boat left the dock it let out another huge blast from its steam whistle that scared us all and spooked the horses again. The animals went galloping over fields and meadows and along the grassy river bank. So again our drivers had to go chasing after them.

This happened on many mornings: the boat bellowed and the horses spooked. The animals never did get used to the sound, at least not all of them. The wiser animals did adjust when they noticed that nothing bad followed the blast, but the dumber animals never did. So we had to order the boatmen not to blow the whistle at all.

We were in Unnunkoski for two weeks, until the sixteenth of November. The women of the village made Karelian rice pastries and other foods of theirs, some kind of barley cakes or whatever, and sold them to us. We wondered a bit about the selling at first. If their men had come to Ostrobothnia to defend it we wouldn't have stooped to taking money for the near-beer broth or dumplings. We would rather have given them for free. We came to the conclusion that trading was so ingrained in the Karelians' blood that it outweighed hospitality. And we did have money. At the end of October, we had been given our army pay and of course we all had our own money too. We weren't short of cash, so we weren't all that put off by the Karelians' business dealings.

Regarding our first army pay, we agreed that everyone would turn over two days' worth of it to the defense forces so they could buy weapons and ammunition and other equipment for us. Every last man of us contributed. There really wasn't any place to spend money, since the army saw to our actual upkeep. Card-playing never became the rage in the Winter War that it did in the other war, when many of the boys were totally hooked on it.

The boys from Jurva came up with a scheme for the contributions: they put the money into a company fund so they themselves could decide what to do with it. The others gave the money directly to the armed forces, even the men from Laihia. The men from Jurva bought all kinds of things with their fund. Many of us started to envy them, they could buy for their company things the rest of us lacked.

The Karelians made coffee for us and sold it by the cupful. There wasn't time to set up a USO in Unnunkoski; we didn't get one until we were in Konnitsa. Time tended to drag here for a grown-up, although the Army tried to organize all sorts of pastimes. They had us drill saluting, which a soldier always needs and which he tends to forget.

In the woods back of Unnunkoski we trained how to attack and defend and withdraw, each company in its own sector, while the battalion commander rode around on horseback seeing to it that the training was carried out according to regulations. Matti Laurila also rushed around the terrain, even though his sore back bothered him badly in the autumn weather. He had hurt it as a young infantryman in Germany, where they'd had them carrying huge logs for building dug-outs somewhere during the First World War.

Then they put us to work making fortifications. We dug trenches and built obstacles against enemy tanks. They were never needed. The enemy didn't come that way, but we couldn't know that at the time. The work was not hard, it was more of a pastime. It was also to pass the time that our drivers started to plow the fields of the Unnunkoski farms. The fall plowing had been far from finished when the men left. We tried to be of help to the people there.

VI

While at Unnunkoski we had time to take the river boat to Käkisalmi, leaving in the morning and coming back in the evening. We had the company commander's permission to go. It was a beautiful town near the shore of Lake Ladoga. We went to look at the Lake too, which was as large as the sea and free of ice. Later on during the winter we would get to see it frozen over from our positions at the mouth of the Taipale River.

We had no reason for going to Käkisalmi. It was just that time passed slowly in Unnunkoski on Sunday when the Army had arranged no pastime except for field church services. They were held frequently during the week too.

In Käkisalmi we took in the ways of the Karelians, trying to figure out what kind of people they really were. At home we had only heard talk about them. I have to say that they were really peculiar. Sometimes we were almost ashamed of the talk and fuss and needless bustle that we saw in Käkisalmi. We didn't care to go there again even if we could have so we began spending our free time in our quarters. We made hill bands for our horses at Unnunkoski, or rather our company shoemaker made them to a pattern the Karelians gave us. We guessed that we would not be in Unnunkoski forever.

We had to build armored vehicle traps at Unnunkoski, quarrying huge slabs of stone which we set up to stop the armor. There were strict orders and directives from the regiment about the kind of stone slabs we were to use and how they were to be situated on the terrain to do the most damage to the tanks. But we got no drills to use on the rocks although we asked for them over and over again. We learned that in the army orders flow freely from above, that telephone lines are kept busy with orders, but that it was impossible for us to get practical tools even by begging. In the end it bugged us so much we went and bought iron bars from a store in Unnunkoski. Our smiths tempered them into rock drills for us. We also got the engineers to split the rocks for us with picric acid. And so we got enough of the slabs for the tank traps. They were never needed, in that war or in the later one. We carried three-meter high stone slabs into people's fields and stuck them up there in long rows for nothing. They may still be there for all I know. Or maybe the Russian boys carried them away from the kolkhoz fields they now have in Unnunkoski, back to the woods where we first quarried and dragged them out.

At first we were lodged in tents but then they moved us into houses, where the bedbugs and cockroaches were such a plague that the whole company was soon scratching itself with all the claws of both hands. Bedbug bites itch like mad and it's no fun to have cockroaches as live-in buddies. Those vermin spread a rash to the whole battalion that made us miserable. Many of us got fed up with the troubles on this war-jaunt. We made up all kinds of excuses for home leave, but none were granted at Unnunkoski. Paavo and I tried to come up with a reason, but couldn't do it. We didn't want to tell our superiors outright lies. It was like that in those days. Many hoped we could come to some kind of agreement with the Russians, that the future would be a little brighter and not so completely dark. Because of the rash the whole battalion was forbidden to use the sauna, which was a severe blow to us. Going to the sauna was one of the few enjoyable pastimes we had.

The ban on saunas did nothing to raise our spirits, nor did the fact that we were ordered back into the tents because of the bedbugs and cockroaches. It was already nearing the end of October. It wasn't winter yet, but the weather was chilly and raw, and a building is always more comfortable at night than a canvas tent, no matter how much good birch wood you use to heat it.

VII

I was on guard duty when word came down that the regiment, including the second battalion, would be moved to another place. Our platoon leader came to the guard post to round us up.

It was already getting dark when he marched us to the tents. The boys were throwing their goods together and loading them on wagons. Paavo had stowed my things into my pack and set it at the foot of a tree outside the tent. As we came up, the boys were already carrying out the center pole of the tent. They collapsed it, folded it up, and put it on the wagon.

The platoon leader gave us our marching orders, and we heard we were going to the village of Konnitsa in Pyhäjärvi. The weather had turned cold in early November; there had been frost and the roads were frozen. When we set out on the march, it began to rain, not a heavy rain, only a slow drizzle. From where the tents had been we marched to the road, through the village of Unnunkoski, and onto the Pyhäjärvi road. People came out of their houses to say goodbye and wish us and our country the best of luck. We had gotten to know many of them during our stay in their village, and our country's cause was something we had in common.

The rain soaked the road so much that the footing was soon

slippery. We practically had to hold on to the horses to keep them on the road. The boys had tried to find spiked nails in stores and army supplies for the horseshoes, but none were to be found. On the way to Unnunkoski we'd had to push the horses and wagons on the uphill and hold them back on the downhill; now we also had to hold the horses from either side to keep them from slipping into the ditch, for the road was so slippery and icy. And we ourselves had a job staying on the road. Those who weren't pushing the horses or keeping them on the road made the whole trip holding on to one another, three or four men abreast.

The march to Konnitsa was not as long as the march from the Inkilä station to Unnunkoski, but in the dark and rain, it was no fun. No one could ride the officers' horses on that footing. My brother had a fever, but he marched along with the rest of us. He had gotten chilled during the training at Unnunkoski. He'd had only one layer of clothing with him then, had been badly soaked during some attack drill in the woods, and had not been able to dry off until he was back in quarters that evening. He got ill from that.

We'd spent many days building tank traps along the road to Pyhäjärvi, but when we marched off, it was already so dark we couldn't see our handiwork. And there was little chance to search them out — staying on the road was a full-time job.

Later in the evening it became pitch-dark. No lights were allowed in the marching unit. Traveling became a matter of fumbling our way. You could only guess what was ahead from the noise a large, moving group makes — the sound of walking, the rattle of weapons and equipment, and the noise of the vehicles. The rifles and packs began to weigh on a man's shoulders and was uncomfortable. A gun never does fit a man's back and neck bones, it doesn't sit well there. Nor does a pack fit the shape of a man's back when it's stuffed with all that a man needs on the way to war.

As a joke, someone suggested that we sing, but no one liked the idea, not even the men from Härmä. The company commander told us just to see to it that we and the horses stayed on the road.

We got to Konnitsa at three in the morning. The column stopped and from up front word was passed down from man to man that we had arrived. All the buildings in the village were so blacked out that we didn't even know we were in a village until we got word of it. Then a door opened somewhere, throwing a shaft of light into the darkness. We heard the sound of voices, and other shafts of light opened up. Someone took us through the village and into the woods behind it. The command group had pitched tents there earlier, which had been heated for the whole evening. We went to sleep.

VIII

Our battalion took up residence in this village of Konnitsa; other battalions of Laurila's regiment were also billeted there and in neighboring villages. The accommodations were good enough for even a long stay.

We listened to the Moscow negotiations on radios which the Lotta organizations had sent us from Ostrobothnia. After listening to the Finnish broadcasts we turned to the radio news from Sweden, where they seemed to know somewhat more than the Finns. Of course we listened to more than the news broadcasts. We could not think far into the future during the time we were at Konnitsa. Either war would break out or peace would be preserved; not knowing which we could make no lasting plans. Mostly we lived one day at a time.

We tried to make life at Konnitsa bearable, even comfortable to some extent. Every company tried to upgrade its lodgings, to build rifle and pack racks in them, and provide them with other such war-time home-industry furnishings. The men from Jurva were lodged in the Konnitsa youth club, and every man-jack from Jurva is a woodworker. They began to turn the youth club into a fancy dwelling. They had a lot of money in their company fund, money they collected from their first army pay at Unnunkoski, that the rest of us had given to the Armed Forces for guns and ammunition. Well, these Jurva men bought lumber from a sawmill and other stuff from stores and made that youth club into something grand. They built bunks to sleep on, with nice carvings for the sides like those on a distaff; they made tables for themselves, and chairs, and easy chairs, and framed pictures for the walls and carved all kinds of decorations. The people of Konnitsa no longer recognized their youth club when they went there.

Around the middle of November, when it looked as if the Russians didn't dare face off with us, the people of Konnitsa began returning to their homes. The thought then was that it was the thing to do. The negotiations were continuing and we lived in good faith. Even Swedish radio no longer warned us of the safety zone around Leningrad the Russians needed. On the south shore of the Baltic, that zone probably reached all the way to Warsaw by then. So the people of Konnitsa came back to live in peace in their own areas. They all admired the woodworking skills of the men from Jurva: Jurva has always had plenty of good woodworkers.

But our bosses began to look at the Jurva men's lodgings in the youth club and to think the men had it too good there in their fine quarters. Officers from higher up came to check our lodgings and the defensive installations we were building in the vicinity of Konnitsa. They too thought the men from Jurva, ordinary soldiers, were living as if they were in a luxury hotel. In their opinion the men were living better than the commander of the whole army corps. At first our officers were proud of the fact that there were able and creative men in the regiment, but they realized there was something wrong with the situation when they were told that often enough. That's what we were told.

So our officers decided to take the youth club away from the men of Jurva and establish an officers' club there where they could lead a gentlemanly life suitable to their rank when off duty, and entertain the officers of other units. The battalion was ordered to evict the Jurva men from the youth club and lodge them in army tents, and to give the youth club to the officers, who better understood the worth of such a place. But it never became an officers' club. The men from Jurva raised a real ruckus and then the reserve officers — there were many in our regiment — began to side with them. They said they didn't need any club. The only thing they needed was leave papers and a pass for a train headed for Ostrobothnia. They had clubs enough there in their own home towns. Even the regular army brass came to realize you couldn't push around a bunch of men like that, men from many call-up groups, the way you could a scared company of recruits. They began to ponder a way of retracting the order without losing face or giving the men and non-coms the notion that they had made the bosses back down. They suspected that would be bad for morale and damaging to discipline.

For many days they wrangled over whether the Konnitsa youth club would become an officers' club or continue to house the men of Jurva, who did not budge in their stand. They said they would defend the club against the brass with gun in hand if need be, and no one really wanted a war within our own ranks when we actually were next to the border waiting for an attack from our arch-enemy.

So the officers came up with the idea of turning the youth club into a soldiers' canteen and driving the men from Jurva out to sleep in tents. Naturally everyone wanted a canteen, and the Jurva men no longer had the support of other companies, so they had to leave the youth club. Deep down we had been of the opinion that they were living a little too grandly in the youth club while we had to crouch in our tents or outbuildings or louse-infested houses. But the move into tents rankled to the extent that in leaving the youth club, the men of Jurva ripped out all the pretty decorations and whatever they had made or bought with their own money, taking anything they could pry loose to their tents. And those tents did look grand. There was every imaginable kind of decorative thing in them, carved coat racks and poster beds and bunks with wood carvings at their heads like those in the local museum. Those men from Jurva could make a man out of wood, if need be.

And so the youth club was turned into a canteen for the soldiers, and Lottas came from Ostrobothnia to run it. It became a very enjoyable and popular place. We all went there often. The Lottas fixed it up nicely and boys from all of the companies helped with the decoration. It was a sort of pastime to talk to these women, a way to keep in touch with the softer feminine sex.

Before the canteen opened it had been the custom to have evening prayer in every company around seven or eight: a couple of hymns were sung and someone gave a devotional talk and said an evening prayer. All the men in the company had always taken part in the evening devotions, or at least almost all of them, for the mood of the troops was devout. Everyone had vowed to resist the Russians to the death; in such a state of mind a person readily turns for support to the Highest. But when the canteen opened, the evening devotionals had to be canceled in all the companies. The men were in the canteen drinking coffee the Lottas made, and they liked chatting with the girls better than listening to pious speeches at the evening devotionals. They did attend the religious services held on Sunday during the time when the canteen was closed. And one could still find many among the men whose state of mind was devout; they were quite serious, because nobody was sure what the future would bring. Rumors were always flying and we heard news on the radio that did not make us happy. No one could know if he would go back to Osrobothnia from the song-lands of Karelia on his own two feet or be brought home in a wooden overcoat.

IX

When there was no word of a war, the Karelians began returning to their land and homes. It was about the middle of November when the people of Konnitsa came back. We had to give up all our quarters in the houses and go back to living in tents.

Autumn dragged on slowly, and although the weather was sometimes cold and it snowed, we had rain too. We were still waiting for winter. The people returned to the village, the women and children and the old. The men were all away getting extra training, each one with his own unit. The Karelian units were stationed near the border parishes and the men of the house kept coming on home leave and probably on regular furloughs, since we were doing nothing critical during those weeks. It was mostly shovel work. We built obstacles for the Russian tanks and dug trenches and built log dugouts for our own troops. The men of Konnitsa found it hard to understand why we were digging these holes in their fields while they were doing the same thing a couple of parishes away. We too found it hard to understand why they didn't take us straight to the border and leave them in their own parish. Sometimes we wondered too if we weren't giving ourselves a bloody nose by putting war emplacements under the noses of the Russians as if challenging them. Last summer when

44

the university students had been working on the border fortifications, they had written defiant messages on them, threats stating that this was not a good place for the Russians to come through to try and enslave free Finland. That they would lose their lives if they try. The men from Konnitsa told us about these inscriptions on their visits home. Though none of us trusted much in the Russian desire for peace at the time.

These men of *The Isthmus* were really a cheerful and pleasant bunch, but we could see they didn't like our living with their wives for weeks on end while they themselves were at Kiviniemi, Rautu and Metsäpirtti digging trenches and setting up rocks in fields as tank obstacles. But no big quarrels or fights arose between us while we were in the village of Konnitsa. We don't know what they might have said to their wives and daughters within their own four walls; we were never there to hear it, but the longer we were there, the more distrustful the Karelian men became. They could never sort out why we should be spending weeks with their women both day and night, been dragged from Ostrobothnia to defend their province and all of Finland.

All sorts of things did happen too. We had been away from home for a month and a half and we were young men with the needs of young men, other needs than laying down our lives on the altar of the fatherland. But no great fuss was raised about the satisfaction of those needs; they were handled in a practical way, as it should be in such a poor little village. Then at the Taipale River, especially when we were not actually on front-line duty but in rest areas, many a boy began for some odd reason to remember the girls and wives of Konnitsa and many of them had their addresses in their notebooks. Many of the women had also written poems and verses in the notebooks about the stolen moments they'd shared before the war began. In February the papers of a boy who fell at the Taipale River came into my hands and I took a look at the snatches of verse in his notebook and at the name and address of a girl from Konnitsa. One of them stuck in my mind — it was so nicely written. I don't remember the girl's name, but her name and address were there, and after it the boy himself had written:

> *"You robbed my breast of its peace*
> *you stole my love in fun*
> *and so on."*

I burned the notebook at the Taipale River, I couldn't see sending it home along with the other papers. I felt that his wife at home would have enough grief when the news of his death was brought to her, without adding to it with such useless papers. We all understand that young men and women will talk to each other about other matters than war and country when they have to live in close quarters for weeks on end and meet each other daily, the husbands of the village wives were away for a long time, and our women were hundreds of kilometers away and there was no certainty that we would ever see them again. And many of our boys never did get to see their homefolks again.

Other, less romantic things happened with these Karelian women. The boys in the first battalion were buying milk from a farm and as the weeks went by, it began to seem more and more watery to them. They wondered if it was an omen of war when the butterfat in the milk fell off so drastically. The commander of the first battalion took a sample of the milk to the Käkisalmi cooperative dairy, and on testing there, it was ascertained that the farm wife was extending the milk by pouring water into it. But that she always sent good milk to the dairy. There was no way of knowing how long she had been selling the watered-down milk, but the boys felt that it had been getting more watery all the time. The woman had gotten greedy.

Our boys didn't really like being sold the watered-down stuff at the price of milk. They started to get really angry and planned very carefully how to scare this woman and make the woman answer for her deeds and pay back the money the battalion had paid. But the woman was already frightened when the battalion commander showed her the paper with the results of the dairy tests. She made a special trip to ask forgiveness of the boys, assuring them that the fortunes of the fatherland was important to her too. She served them coffee and coffee-bread, and the boys didn't bother to make a big case of the diluted milk. Both sides agreed to forget the matter forever, and the boys promised not to bear a grudge against the woman.

Nothing like that happened to our battalion. We were satisfied with our food and with what we were able to buy from the farms and stores with our own money. Time dragged on, and we began to think of heading for home, if only someone would give us permission.

X

In Konnitsa, we took life one day at a time. Toward the end of November everyone began making up all sorts of excuses for home leave so we could get back to Ostrobothnia and see our families. Even more we wanted to get away from *The Isthmus* and from the everlasting waiting for war or peace and from building those fortifications. We never knew if they would be used or not, and our work was now mostly a matter of leaning on our crowbars. But the brass were still strict about the leaves. Actually not a single one was issued.

A child was born to one of the men, but he was not allowed to go home, not even for the christening. There was a radio program to which families could send news of happenings at home; that's how he learned he had become a father. He must have been waiting for the news, though. They teased him a lot about having fathered a child. Things like that were on our minds around the end of November. Only after the shots at Mainila, when the negotiations in Moscow were broken off, did we become more serious and start thinking again of our country's affairs and wondering if we would clash with the Russians and how that would turn out.

Then the war did come. On the last day of November the Russians crossed the border at Metsäpirtti and Rautu and began coming into Finland, bombing Helsinki and other places. We didn't know at first what this meant and how far the Russians would go. We were told that the border troops had stopped the Russians at Rautu and Metsäpirtti and on the whole Isthmus and north of it, but the outbreak of war had little effect on our work. We were in Konnitsa and we dug trenches and built tank traps.

There were more religious services and the boys went to them willingly, except in the evening when we preferred to sit in the canteen listening to the radio and talking to the Lottas.

While working on the fortifications we were given new anti-aircraft instructions. Ack-ack squads were put together from the machine-gun companies, with the task of shooting down Russian planes if they tried to fly over Konnitsa to bomb the homeland or to attack our fortification work. Riflemen were also trained in shooting at these planes. At work now we had our rifles and live ammunition with us at all times. But we never got a single chance to shoot at Russian planes in Konnitsa. One stormy day when it was snowing, we heard the sound of a formation of planes flying somewhere. Were they our own planes or the enemy's? We never did find out. We did see Russian planes a few times, but they never dared come within firing range.

As soon as the war started, rumors began to spread. Almost everyone pretended to know what was happening at the front, on *The Isthmus* and farther north. Although the command forbade the spreading of rumors, of course the boys talked among themselves — and who can always tell fact from rumor? It was said that Sweden was already declaring war on Russia, or that America was coming to our aid because it did not approve of such attacks on small, independent countries. At the time, many of the men believed the story about America. I did too.

49

We did get reliable information too. We knew that the Russians drove us quickly back from Metsäpirtti, that our delaying troops were already forced back across the Taipale River in early December, and that they stopped there for a breather, the attacker and the Finn. On the first and second of December the Russians tried in dead earnest to cross the river, but they were stopped. We were told that the Russians started out across the ice-free river in rowboats as if they were coming into their own land, and that there were lots of them. They were without any protection and there was no attempt to give them artillery support for the crossing. They shoved their boats into the water and the men sat down in them and started rowing as if they were on a berry-picking trip. Our men sat behind a ridge of earth on the river bank and when the river was black with Russians, they started firing. It was a great shock to the Russians. They had been told they would be received on the Finnish side as liberators, as men who would free the people from capitalist oppression. When the Finnish machine guns began to sing their harsh song from the earthen ridge on the river, the Russians realized they'd been fed false information. A lot of them died in that river.

The ministers of the Terijoki puppet government along with other Finns who had moved to Russia after the rebellion of 1918 and their propaganda men had assured the Russians that mostly there would be brass brands and little pigtailed girls with flowers to greet them in Finland. The brass bands and pigtailed girls never showed up. Instead our boys mowed them down on that river and their boats sank. Those who were not shot, drowned. The Taipale River carried their bodies into Lake Ladoga. Any who managed to get back to their own shore knew what their reception would be. So did their leaders. So now the Russians

50

really began to marshal their forces before again starting a triumphal march to Helsinki.

They told us about this as we dug trenches at Konnitsa or lay in the tents at night and waited for what they would do with us in the war. The boys talked about our being the headquarters reserve, about how the men of Ostrobothnia would be sent to straighten things out when the situation got very rough at some place along the front where the Finns were not able to resist the Russians. I don't know if it was true, but there was a lot of this kind of talk.

Mannerheim had been made commander of the army as soon as the war broke out, and our company, at least, greeted the news with three cheers. We trusted Mannerheim. We felt that with him as commander of the Armed forces and Matti Laurila as commander of our regiment, *The Isthmus* would be a tough place for the Russians to begin their conquest of Finland.

We had to wait until Independence Day before they began to miss us on the battlefield. Until then, we prepared defenses at Konnitsa. On Independence Day we moved out. Before leaving, Laurila had the whole regiment parade. We assembled in a field behind the youth club, where the regimental commander gave a speech. Then the chaplain spoke and we sang a couple of hymns.

Thinking about it later, it seemed rash for Laurila to mass all his men in a wide-open field, hold them there for more than an hour, and even have them pass in review. If a Russian pursuit plane had come over, it would have left ugly tracks. But there was a little storm, and no enemy plane appeared. We had known about the parade and the assembly for departure the day before. A Russian spy would have had plenty of time to get word to his superiors that the men of Ostrobothnia were in a field behind the

Konnitsa Youth Club, an easy target, but apparently no one did because no planes appeared during all that rigmarole. We'd been hunting spies continually at Konnitsa, there were constant warnings about them, and the boys did nab one, the manager of the cooperative store.

But the spies sent no information about this parade to the Russian side, and we were able to march past Matti Laurila undisturbed by airplanes. The march of a large group of men like that is always a great sight and a morale-builder, and those who took part in it were sure the Russians had better not try anything big with us without a lot of back-up. Matti Laurila understood that part of a soldier's inner life. He'd had Jaeger training in Germany.

In the evening the regiment marched out of Konnitsa, at least a part of it did. A part of it got to ride on trucks. We didn't know where we were going, but later we found out that it was to the Taipale River.

We marched two days to the Taipale River, two days and two nights; at times we tried to get some sleep in army tents and houses, but it was no rest for us. Cold and tired, we all tried to doze wherever we could.

We were put in reserve behind a regiment from Central Finland a couple of kilometers back of the front lines. We could hear the crunching of artillery all the time.

On the morning of December ninth we got to see for the first time what this modern war was like and what effect artillery has. The Russians had brought quite a few artillery pieces and heavy mortars to the other side of the Taipale River, and they were firing at us from in back of Igolka Point with the guns of two warships, at us and at the front line, and they did not spare their ammunition. They fired as fast as they could, with pin-point accuracy at the front line and with more scattered searching fire here in the rear area where we were.

During those first days we lay in foxholes we had dug for ourselves at Linnanka on the shores of Ladoga. The black earth there was chopped up by the artillery, so pitted and muddy that at first our snow uniforms were the only white splotches on it. Soon they too were muddy and black. We knew so little about unexploded shells that in the evening the boys would carry them into the tents on their shoulders to take them home as war souvenirs. Soon that was forbidden and we were given directions on what to do with these duds. The engineers came to detonate them, and we did it ourselves too. In general there were lots of duds among the Russian shells, on some days over half of them. It took us a while to learn all the different tricks of this war trade, and the demands it put on a man.

The Russian searching fire took the first of our boys while we were there in reserve for the men from Central Finland. A few were killed by shell fragments. Many others were only wounded. It was around the tenth of December that we lost the first boys. It was only then that we began to understand what the war might bring to each of us. The dead were well known to us. They were all from our home parish, we had lived side by side with them for a couple of months, and now suddenly they were gone. Only the body was left.

We talked a lot about the first men who died. We recalled everything about them, tried to think only good of them, to remember situations where they had shone to advantage. Later, when we were losing many boys, there was no longer time to react in the same way.

We were allowed to stay in rear-area reserve for a week. Already by mid-December being in reserve meant lying in our holes by day waiting for a command to counterattack, and spending nights in the front-line trenches digging them deeper, throwing out the bodies of Russians, carrying our own men's bodies back from the front lines, heaping the sand thrown into the trenches by the artillery back onto the banks, and reinforcing the trenches with sandbags. Being in reserve was no longer any kind of rest at all.

We were switched to the front lines on December sixteenth. Or on the evening of the sixteenth. The men from Central Finland went back to rest. It was a dark, cloudy night. We didn't know where on the Taipale River front we would wind up — men were not given this kind of information in advance — but as we dug out collapsed sections of trenches in the sector, we knew it was a nasty place. There were no nice places.

XI

When morning dawned we saw the kind of place we had been brought to: the fields of Terenttilä, the Schoolhouse Woods, the Pärssinen Woods and the Taipale River in back of them. Beyond the fields of Terenttilä were the Russian tanks. We counted ten of them. The Russian artillery kept up a steady fire. It had been firing since the small hours of the morning, but the shells were going over us and landing somewhere behind the front line. Only in daylight did they begin firing out in front of us. We kept watching the tanks to see what the Russians had in mind. They were driving back and forth beyond the field a half-kilometer away; foot soldiers were moving around there too. Our own artillery fired a few rounds at them.

At about ten the tanks came up to the tank traps and thrashed around there. There was no infantry with them, so we had little to do. Our fire had no effect on them. The boys did fire their rifles at them, even blazed away with machine guns, but that did no good. The Russians drove their tanks through the field up to our tank traps and used their treads to break the traps, the barbed-wire entanglements, and the mounted coils set up to protect our position. When they moved they made the kind of racket that two poorly joined pieces of metal make. We could hear that things were loose somewhere, very loose. The company commander sent word to the battalion that there was work for anti-tank men out in front of our positions and soon an anti-tank gun and its crew did arrive. Before their gun was set up, the tanks turned, drove back across the Terenttilä fields toward the Taipale River, and disappeared into the river channel or behind its sloping banks.

Our whole company was on line. We sat or lay at the bottom of the trenches under the Russian artillery fire. During this barrage we all realized for the first time that the Russians were trying to hit and kill us. We knew that the artillery fire in the rear had been random, but now everyone knew just what the Russians were firing at. It made everything clear suddenly. And all this time we kept trying to see what the Russians were up to on the other side of the field. It was thirty below, but not one of us was cold, there was so much adrenalin in our blood.

Soon we saw the Russians line up their tanks, with infantry grouped behind each one. The men had machine guns equipped with metal shields. Men and machines started out across the field, the tanks driving abreast and the infantry following, dragging and pushing the machine guns. The tanks were going so fast that the infantry had to trot to keep up. The artillery kept firing at us until the tanks were halfway across the field, then shifted their fire to behind us, to the service of supply and the headquarters. We tried to call in to our artillery, but all the wires were cut. Someone had to run into that artillery fire to ask our own guns for a protective concentration on the Russians. But they weren't able to respond.

We had to take off our gloves and start firing. The tanks drove toward our positions with the long overcoats running and dying behind them. They really had no shelter. Machine guns picked them off like grouse, and they fell and lay there in the field at

Terenttilä. Machine guns and automatic rifles raked their ranks wickedly, and Russians fell in the field and into its drainage ditches. Heedless of anything, the tanks kept coming, turning only at the obstacles in front of our positions. There were no longer any infantrymen with them. They had all fallen.

The anti-tank men set fire to one tank with their gun, and it was left burning on a barbed-wire barrier. The other tanks turned back and started driving toward the Taipale River. Our own artillery fired a strike at the field, but the tanks were already out of sight behind the river bank or in the woods near Pärssinen.

We figured that the Russians had had enough for that day, since they had lost one tank, and boys from the steppes lay scattered around the field like brown lumps, lots of them. Our own artillery fired a strike into the Pärssinen woods, since it was thought to be an assembly area for the Russian tanks, but when the artillery strike ended we started to hear a heavy rattle of small arms fire from the woods. Then a command came down from Laurila that we were not to attack into the Schoolhouse Woods or the Pärssinen woods so as not to inflict losses on our own men. Shortly we got word from battalion that some of our men were still in those woods, left there the previous night when we'd tried to take the area. They had not been able to break out. Word came that they would come out as soon as it was dark, along with a plea that our own artillery not fire on them. They had attacked the woods at night and been separated from each other in the dark. Platoon leaders and men had been killed, for the Russians had had time to bring in automatic weapons and dig in. When their platoon and squad leaders were killed, the boys started running across the clearing to their own lines. The Russians shot many of them in the field and at the barbed-wire entanglements. Boys were left hanging on the barbed wire, and in the morning the Russian machine guns had blown them off it like a big wind before their bodies could be brought back. The rest of the boys had stayed in Pärssinen waiting for morning — a messenger brought word from there.

The Russian artillery began to hammer our lines again, and we saw tanks drive into an open line across the Terenttilä field. Men in long overcoats formed up behind them, infantrymen. We figured that today's war work wasn't over yet, that maybe it was only half begun.

They started to come out again. The tanks pulled sleds with infantry sitting on them and others half-running behind them. We had to start shooting them again. Our signal corps men had got a line in to the artillery fire observer, but before he could contact the battery the line was cut again. Lines that ran along the ground could not withstand the awful churning of the Russian artillery. Again the Russian infantry began falling in the field and from off the sleds behind the tanks to lie motionless in the snow.

The Russians fired mortars into our positions and our boys started dying when they had to stand up in the foxholes to shoot at the Russian infantry with the tank and mortar shells falling the whole time into our positions and in front of and behind them. The medics bandaged the wounded and hauled them on Lapland sleds back to the Pihkahovi area, where the unit's first-aid station was. The dead were left to wait for the coming of darkness. They had time to wait.

The Russian tanks drove right up to our barbed-wire entanglements. The infantry did not follow them, but turned around in the middle of the field and ran back toward the Taipale River. One of the tanks was hit by an anti-tank gun at a barbed-wire barrier and

58

was left there. The boys destroyed another tank with a satchel charge; they came up from their rifle pit with the charge, rolled over and crawled close to the tank and managed to hurl the satchel charge on top of it. There were two of them, and they both came back unharmed. The other tanks turned around and headed for their homeland and caught up to their own infantry in the field. As they all tried to get into the river channel at Sikiö Point, our artillery fired a strike into their midst. A lot of the infantry-men were left there. One of the tanks caught fire and burned in the field for a long time, smoke rising from it the whole after-noon. The wounded groaned in the field, and a few of the long overcoats tried to crawl toward the Taipale River for shelter. We shot them with our rifles.

We started to get hungry. An order came from regiment that we were to dig a common grave in the Pärssinen woods where some of our own dead lay, and that we were to take the whole woods and hold it. We began to search around to see how we might dig a grave like that into frozen ground with shovels and crowbars.

While we were planning how to dig the grave, we saw a group of men the size of a platoon coming toward us from Pärssinen. They came running across the field. We waited for the Russians to start mowing them down, but there was no firing at all from their side. The boys were able to run across the whole field. They jumped into our trench and lay resting on its bottom; running in thick clothing with their heavy equipment had worn them out.

They were led by a second lieutenant. He said that under orders he had led the men out of Pärssinen, where they had lain for a day and a night under the fire of their own and enemy artillery, keeping the Russians at bay. He was told that he should not have brought his men out of Pärssinen, that he should have waited there for us to dig the common grave and then come to help him. He did not intend to go back. Now the Russians began to thump our positions with their artillery, but they had begun firing too late. The boys had crossed the field and were safe in our trenches. The Russians were not able to keep up the fire for long. The second lieutenant went to take the platoon to his own company, the fifth. He asked us to let the battalion know that there was not a single one of our men left alive in Pärssinen.

We were ordered to open up the trenches hammered by the Russian artillery. We shoveled out the sand from their bottoms and reinforced the sides with logs and sandbags. The company commander came to check our work and told us that the fifth company boys had been ordered to attack Pärssinen again. We were to follow the progress of their attack from the side and shoot any Russians who might try to cross in front of us to help their comrades. Soon we saw the fifth company boys rise from the trenches and run across the field toward Pärssinen. There was a platoon of them. There was no firing from the Russians. Soon the men disappeared into the woods and remained there. I don't know why the Russians didn't try to shoot them out in the field.

The Russian artillery did not fire on Terenttilä that afternoon. From other directions we heard the firing of artillery, mortars, and small arms, but no fire at all came to our positions.

XII

The engineers arrived in the evening, some thirty men with horses and sleighs. They had anti-tank and infantry mines with them. The men driving the horses ran off as soon as the sleighs were unloaded. The engineers called the battalion about it, since the telephone connection was working again, then stood beside their stacks of mines and waited while their platoon leader was out studying the terrain in front of us for the best places to start laying the mines. The men were from Järvenkylä. They said that they had gone from Rautu to Kiviniemi at the start of the war, and from Kiviniemi over the Vuoksi River. They'd been ordered to build an infantry bridge over it and had ferried Second Lieutenant Blick's troops across. Then they had destroyed the highway bridge there, as well as their own. They had burned the villages of Vaalimo and Arkuntanhu. The Russians had bombed Kiviniemi severely from the air and had tried to destroy the highway bridge, but had not scored a single hit on it. When they stopped bombing, the engineers themselves blew up both bridges. The entire highway bridge had dropped into the river.

They also told us that Russian tanks had driven onto their mines at Kiviniemi and caught fire. The men were trapped inside the tanks and burned there. We told them we had destroyed a few tanks that day just for the heck of it when we were repelling an infantry attack.

The engineering platoon leader came back from surveying the ground with our company commander and went to call battalion. They had not found a good place for laying mines to block the enemy advance. The engineers were ordered to take them to the Sixth Company's position which the Russian infantry and tanks could more easily breach, and where the mines could be put to better use. The engineers went to search for the drivers but did not find them. Then the leader of the engineering platoon and our company commander went to look for the drivers. Our CO ordered our platoon to set up the night watch and sent the other men into the log dugouts.

The engineers came into the dugouts too, to warm up and wait for the horses and drivers to be found. It was late evening when they left. At about eight o'clock, a propaganda truck drove up in back of our positions and began shouting something in Russian which we could not understand. We went out to listen and see if this kind of war-making had any effect on the Russians, but had to leave in haste because the Russians immediately got a fix on the loudspeaker truck and fired long and earnestly on it and our positions. The shouting in Russian was drowned out by the roar of the cannon and the explosion of the shells. The propaganda truck drove away as soon as the artillery fire began, but we had to go into our dugouts and lie there afraid that we would take a direct hit. Those dugouts were not built to take one.

They say that in the Joensuu sector during the early days of the war heavy artillery had scored a direct hit on a dugout, killing thirty of our boys. It wasn't nice to hear such stories.

Later that evening when the artillery barrage had ended, a

messenger brought a written message from the regiment that a propaganda truck was coming up in back of the lines to transmit propaganda in Russian. We were told to beware of artillery barrages which might ensue. A barrage did follow. The Russians chewed up our positions for over an hour. All we could do was sit in the dugout and hang on. The earth shook, the dugout rocked, and mud, earth, and sand splattered through the hastily fitted logs onto the floor. Every second we survived seemed a small miracle.

My brother and I had the midnight watch. The men we relieved said that they'd kept hearing the sound of motors starting up and the clanking of tank treads in the Schoolhouse Woods. They wondered if the Russians might still start out to conquer Finland that night and told us to listen sharply to every sound so we'd know when the conquest was beginning. My brother and I stood in the pit and listened. We did hear many sounds across the field, and we tried to peer out there to see when our Russian neighbor might start coming so we could alert the boys in the dugout. We agreed that my brother would go to alert them and that I would stay to hold off the Russians. But no matter how hard we stared at the open area we didn't see much. We had no flares at the time and the sky was clouded over. We saw nothing, but we heard sounds beyond the field. The Russians were there.

During the night the platoon leader came to check that we were awake. He asked me to go out in the field with him to see if there were any papers of value to us in the pockets of dead Russians. He also told me that during the day our men had intercepted a radio message ordering the Russian army to continue crushing the Finnish White Guard without mercy, and that we were that White Guard. The message also told the Russians that the Finnish worker was waiting for his Russian brother to free him from the capitalist yoke.

We got out of the rifle pit and started crawling across the field toward the Taipale River. Right outside our barbed-wire barrier was the wreck of the first tank set on fire by a shell, and around it lay the bodies of those who had gotten out of the burning tank and been shot. We turned them over and searched their pockets for papers. They had lain there since morning and were frozen stiff. It was hard to turn them over, the frozen blood made their clothing as hard as sheet metal. The Russians fired a flare and we had to lie motionless among the bodies until the flare died out, afraid that someone would rake the field where we were lying with fire. Then we still had to get back. The platoon leader took all the papers we had found and went into the dugout to check them. Early in the morning when the guard changed and my brother and I went into the dugout to warm up, I saw that my hands were bloody. I tried to wash them in the muddy snow I scooped up in front of the dugout. Inside everybody was asleep. The stench there was awful, wet clothes and foot rags and the smell of drying shoes, and of old food which the Central Finlanders had dumped under the chopped straw on the floor.

There was no light in the dugout except for a kind of lamp that stood on the table. It was a wine bottle, with gasoline as its fuel and its wick a strip of foot rag stuffed into a spent cartridge. It didn't give much light, it just smoked and stank. The men's snoring shook the dugout. That's where we had to sleep. My kid brother slept well; he fell asleep as soon as he lay down. It took me longer to fall asleep. The platoon leader came back from checking the guard and said that yesterday was Sunday, December seventeenth. That didn't seem important.

The platoon leader did not dare sleep the whole night, except for nodding off a bit while sitting. He had to keep going through the trench, waking up the men on watch. Although it was twenty below and the Russian artillery and mortar fire continued all night long and the tanks clanked out there in the darkness of Schoolhouse Woods, the men on watch still could not help falling asleep.

XIII

Early in the morning the engineers came again, waking up everyone who was still asleep in the dugout. They told us they'd been ordered to our company's position again. According to their platoon leader, they'd spent maybe half a year just going back and forth between battalion command and the different companies. But it was not their duty to ask if it made any sense. When our company commander returned, he ordered some men from our dugout to go with the engineers to carry their mines. He described a safe and secure route to the fifth company's position: they were to go through the woods and be wary of the fifth company lookouts who might be jittery because the Russians had visited their barbed-wire barriers late in the evening. The password was "Taipale Battleaxe."

When the men left, we tried to get more sleep, but nothing came of it. There was continual traffic in and out of the dugout. When the guard changed, the men coming off duty insisted on telling us everything they'd heard from the Russian side. So we got up and started talking about things at home.

About six o'clock the platoon leader went to check the watch and to see what the dawn would bring us in Terenttilä. He came back shouting that the Russians were breaking into our positions.

Everyone put on whatever he had time to snatch up, grabbed his gun, and ran toward the place he'd been stationed the day before. The men on guard were firing as fast as they could in the half-darkness of early morning. When we rushed forward we saw that the Russians were already in our foxholes. We couldn't go on, they were firing right into our faces. Those in the lead were killed then and there and even those behind them were hit. Our company commander arrived quickly, and we started trying to figure out how many Russians there were in our foxholes and what we could do about it.

The company commander asked why the men on watch hadn't seen the Russians until they were almost in our foxholes, but there was no one to answer. They were all dead. The platoon leader set a machine gun to singing out in front of our positions so that no more of the boys from the steppes could get into our trenches. The Russians already in the trenches kept firing along them in either direction and trying to advance beyond them. We formed a skirmish line behind the foxholes to stop them from coming farther. A messenger was sent to battalion to explain our situation.

The company commander said we either had to drive the Russians out of our foxholes or kill them on the spot. Just as we were starting to drive them out with machine pistols and hand grenades, a line of them came toward the dugout along a connecting trench. They were right in our faces and the boys fought hand-to-hand with those in front. They hacked at each other with their gun barrels and stocks, with no chance to load or fool around fixing bayonets. The Russians were strong lads and they were afraid of dying. We tossed hand grenades into the trench behind them and shot them from the edge of the trench. We had to fight hand-to-hand with the ones in the lead.

Machine gunners and boys from other platoons controlled the ground out front with their fire so that no more Russian boys could get into the trench. We killed all those who were in it, about a platoon of them. A few got out of the trench and started running across the field to their own lines, but not many made it. It was so easy for our boys to shoot them on the open terrain toward the Taipale River. The day was just dawning. The din ended when all the Russians in the foxholes were dead. Things were quiet now and we had a breathing spell. But soon the Russian artillery opened up. It felt as if they were firing at us with every cannon and mortar they had in Taipale. We had to throw ourselves down on the bottom of a foxhole and lie there for a long time on top of the still warm Russian bodies and the bullet-riddled bodies of our own men, looking into the faces of the dead. There was no time to choose a place. We just had to throw ourselves down when the artillery and mortar barrage began.

As we lay there waiting to die, with the artillery shells bursting on all sides of the foxholes and mortar shrapnel whining through the air, our company commander shouted over the din that the Russians were coming again across the Terenttilä field, with tanks this time, and that there were lots of them. They seemed to have men to spare, and although the air was filled with the sounds of firing and screaming and with flying metal from the shells, we had to get up in order to see over the edge of the foxhole. We had to get our weapons working in all those eruptions of earth and sand caused by the artillery fire. We had to draw a bead on the Russians and shoot them.

When the Russian infantry was halfway across the field, the artillery fire shifted away from us. But now the tanks opened direct-trajectory fire and charged forward again, pounding our positions, filling the air with sand and shell fragments. There were lots of infantry, and they just kept coming, although we fired at them with everything we could get to work. Again long overcoats lay like brown lumps in the field, but the others kept coming on, shouting.

They came right up to our positions. We had to leave, to get out of the trenches and run into the woods, where the platoon leader was already forming a skirmish line. We lay in that line in the shelter of trees and fallen logs, waiting for the Russians to come out of the trench and try to advance. But they did not come. Their tanks had stopped in a row at the barbed-wire barriers and were firing their canon and machine guns to either side and to the place where we lay in back of the trench.

The company commander went along our line asking if we could drive the Russians from the trench once more, but there were too few of us. Our platoon leader didn't think we could get to our position and drive them out. There must have been at least a company of Russians in the position. They were firing as fast as they could, and they had tank support behind the barbed-wire barrier. So the company commander went to round up help from other Finnish units.

The medics gathered the wounded and tried to get them out from under the fire to the rear lines. Our dead were left at our positions. The morning had passed. The Russians did not try to advance beyond the trench. More of their troops tried to join them from in back of the Terenttilä field, but our artillery fire stopped them.

In the afternoon a written order came from battalion that we were to drive out the Russians who had thrust into our positions. We didn't need a written order to tell us that, but there were only a few of us left. So we thought we would at least try to keep the Russians from coming farther than they had that morning. The platoon leader went back to clarify the situation, appointing a squad leader to lead us for the time being. They had received two platoons from Lieksa who were in reserve attached to us, but they were digging another line of defense farther back. They were to help us clear the Russians from our positions.

Evening was already coming on. The company commander ordered as many hand grenades as possible to be brought up. Soon they began arriving. The Russians were firing on us all the while from our positions, but they had no really heavy weapons with them. They were only spattering away with rifles, and their artillery fire was not aimed at our positions. Our boys began heaving hand grenades onto the Russians and the rest of us rushed into the trench from both ends. When we got control of that section of it, the Russian artillery opened fire on our positions, and the Russians had to run off into their own artillery fire. Many of them died there. Running toward home across the field at Terenttilä, they found their deathbed.

We lay in our own trench again and waited for the Russian artillery concentration to slack off enough for us to get into the shelter of the dugout. When the firing ended, we began to clear the foxholes of the dead and the cave-ins. Not a single wounded Russian was left, they were all dead. And we lost a lot of our own boys. From the second platoon of the Lieksa battalion, we found only one who could go back to the reserve area; the others went to the first aid station or to body transport.

Regimental commander Laurila came that evening and ordered the digging work that had to be done the next night. He stopped at every company position and promised that we would get help from the reserve battalion that night. Soon men began to arrive and we were able to start working.

XIV

We dug foxholes the whole night. We had a big argument with the men from the reserve battalion over the digging. They said they had not gotten to sleep for many nights, because they had been clearing out foxholes on the front line every night. They just wanted to sleep. During the day the artillery fire and the explosions of mortar shells had kept them awake. Their officers had brought them here to work and then gone off to sleep in their own quarters. These men refused to listen to another unit's officers. One by one and in small groups they left for their own beds in the darkness of night, leaving the digging to us. Most of them left, but not all of them. Our company commander could do nothing with them, every time he turned his back, men were already in the woods, running in a crouch. You couldn't start shooting them. We couldn't stop them — we didn't have time to. We knew that at dawn the Russians would start firing again, as part of the day's work, and then we had to have a foxhole for everyone to save his life.

Men who had been at listening posts during the night told us they'd heard the Russians driving tanks in the Schoolhouse Woods and running their engines to keep them warm. When our stint on watch came round, Paavo and I took our digging tools to the back of the dugout, went back to the foxhole, got up out of it, and crawled to where the listening post was. Both of the men on watch were asleep, and we had to wake them up. They got up stiff with cold and started toward the dugout. We tried to hear everything that was happening out in front. We could hear the digging in our positions clearly and the sounds from the Russians from farther off beyond the Terenttilä fields and all the way to the Taipale River.

Suddenly we heard heavy fire from infantry weapons out in front of us. There was shouting and the rattle of machine guns and automatic rifles. We hit the ground and tried to take cover, guessing at where the firing was coming from, but in the darkness it wasn't clear. I told Paavo to go to our base and tell them that the Russians were up to something and that the platoon leader should come and check it out. Paavo left, but came back at once, the platoon leader with him. They had met on the way. The three of us listened to where, a short distance away, a tough fight was going on in the darkness. Then there was silence, which lasted until morning. It wasn't until the following morning that we learned that the fifth company had tried to take all of the Pärssinen woods, but it hadn't turned out that way. The Russians had driven them out of the woods. That's what the fighting was about.

Paavo and I stood the rest of the watch recalling everything that had happened the day before and wondering that we were both still standing there in one piece. Paavo remembered how on the march to the Taipale River the whole battalion had stopped at Tykkitie and we'd got the news from somewhere that Hungary and Turkey had joined in the war against Russia the day before. We had given three cheers for the Hungarians and Turks who were now our brothers-in-arms. Paavo wondered where the

Hungarians and Turks could be dilly-dallying, since we would soon need them here at the Taipale River if we kept losing boys at the same rate.

Early in the morning after we had been relieved from guard duty and snatched a few minutes' sleep, the platoon leader came to wake us up. He told us that before daylight we had to make a reconnaissance in force in the Schoolhouse Woods, to look around and calculate how many men and how much military ware the Russians had in store for us there. Some ten of us were picked and the platoon leader himself went to take us into the woods. We made the boys swear not to shoot us on our way back. The platoon leader explained that we were to go into the Schoolhouse Woods, to calculate the strength of the enemy there and the amount of their military gear, and to set fire to the Hiekkala houses. They had been left intact in early December when the border troops and the delaying units had been forced to leave some ground in enemy hands on this side of the Taipale River.

We asked him if the Russians would let us walk across the Terenttilä field to the Schoolhouse Woods to count their troops and material and to light fires on the way back. We didn't think they would, but that didn't help. We had to go.

We tried to sneak out of the trench without being seen by the Russians. A light snow was falling and it was still dark, but it was the kind of darkness you get in the winter. You thought you could see all the time, but you kept falling into shell holes. We knew that the Pärssinen and Schoolhouse Woods were somewhere out there in the darkness, that Hiekkala was to the right, and that the Sikiöniemi houses were before the Schoolhouse Woods. Where the enemy was, we didn't know. That's what we were supposed to find out.

When we began to hear voices ahead of us, we started to crawl. Suddenly the voices were close to us, and we were asked something in a foreign language. When we didn't answer they started shooting at us and we shot back and then we heard someone running. We figured that we had been spotted.

Our platoon leader said we had to try going farther forward to see who had been lying in wait for us. We said the Russians must have had a two-man watch out in front of the lines checking out our nightime chores, just as we had teams out listening for the Russians. The platoon leader said we had to attack now and take the positions where the Russians had been. It would be a disgrace to return to our lines empty-handed.

So we rose and ran and fired and came to the place the Russians had scooted away from. Now their machine guns began to sweep the darkness from beyond the Terenttilä fields. They had tracer bullets, from which we saw that they were firing some hundred meters beyond us. We didn't mind that at all. When the fire came closer, we looked for shell holes for shelter. I happened to be leading the reconnaissance patrol, and as I lay there the platoon leader leapt into the same hole as I. He asked who was there, and I said my name. He asked if I was very scared. I said this was really no fun, but that I wasn't all that scared. He left, and I wondered why he had asked particularly about my being scared. It was only when we got back to our own lines after a couple of hours that I noticed why he had asked. The boys in the dugout told me I stank horribly of human excrement. I started to check myself and came to the conclusion that out in the field in the dark I had jumped into a hole that a pair of Russians on watch had used as a latrine. I was shit from head to foot and it was plainly human shit on my clothes. I was really in a dilemma because there was no way I could change clothes and there was no wash water anywhere. I had to scrape myself clean with a hunting knife.

We gained little in our reconnaissance that night. We never did get close to the Schoolhouse Woods and the Russians had driven our boys out of Pärssinen so we couldn't have gone there. And the Hiekkala houses were left unburned. But we did get out of there and back to the dugout before daylight. Almost immediately after that, the Russians began to press us with their tanks and infantry and artillery. It was a kind of routine production work: they would drive some ten tanks in open formation to the other side of the Terenttilä field, always with some thirty pointy-capped infantrymen behind every tank, and start toward our positions. They had a monotonous way of making war then, in December.

We fought through the morning. Early in the afternoon the Russians stopped making war for the day. Three hundred new bodies lay in front of our positions again, but many of our boys got sent home in pieces too. When the Russians stopped fighting, we started to dig the foxholes open again and to clean our weapons. Food came and we ate.

XV

They brought us milk during the night in twenty-liter cans, the drivers leaving it outside the dugout for us to drink. In the morning the milk was frozen solid. We had to chip off chunks of it with our bayonets and eat the chips or mix them with tea and coffee or melt them in our mess kits over the stove.

While we were cursing the milkmen for not carrying the milk into the dugout, we were called out in a hurry and had to stop melting the milk. We ran from the dugout to the foxholes and looked out to see what was coming toward us from the Terenttilä field today. Morning dawned, but we saw no movement in the field.

We started to wonder if the Russians were taking the day off, since we did not know how long the Russian work-week was. According to our calendar, it was now Wednesday, but last Sunday our leisure had been short. We said that Wednesday would do fine as a holiday for us, when from our positions to the left men began to pour out onto the field. Our own artillery had earlier fired what they called an artillery strike, but to us it sounded like some kind of faint thumping compared to the Russian artillery barrages. Our boys were attacking toward Hiekkala. Later we heard that their objective was to take the Hiekkala houses and set fire to them and then to come back to our side when they had finished the sabotage. We'd had no knowledge of their attack, although we were supposed to have been informed of it during the night. The word got lost somewhere along the way.

They were boys from the ninth company. We watched them rushing across the Terenttilä field toward Hiekkala. Not a pleasant place for that kind of work, I thought. It was already bright daylight. The Russians quickly opened fire on them from a distance, but the boys pushed on doggedly. They advanced in short dashes, lying in shell holes in between, but they did not get to Hiekkala. Men began to fall, killed or wounded. Their platoon leader saw that there was no chance the attack would succeed. We could see that it wouldn't, no matter how many platoons they killed off. The leader ordered the men back to their own lines. Attacking toward Hiekkala was no harder than retreating from it, or rather it was easier, since now they had the dead and wounded with them. They were carrying half the platoon when they came back. We were too far away for our fire to help them, and our artillery was silent, but the Russian artillery was firing for all it was worth, the cannons and mortars. It was a tough spot for the boys, out in that field.

Later we heard that over ten boys had been wounded in the attempt and three killed, all on account of the houses in Hiekkala. They wanted to destroy them so that the Russians could not get warm in them at night. Our own artillery did not have the incendiary shells which could easily have set fire to the houses, so we had to try using men in place of fire bombs. But neither we nor the boys from Company Nine could manage to burn the houses down.

The boys from the Ninth got themselves and their dead and wounded out from under the Russian artillery fire and back to their own lines. When the Russians saw that the field was clear of our men, they turned their cannon on us and let the iron fly full tilt. We lay under that fire, many of us thinking it made no sense to go and harass the Russians for nothing. Better to leave them in peace as long as they stayed in their own positions. We were convinced that we couldn't set fire to the Hiekkala houses except with incendiary shells or aerial bombs.

We wondered too that we never saw our own planes at all. We had seen only one on the seventh day of December when we first came to the Taipale River, and we weren't completely sure even about that. It was a strange-colored pursuit plane and it flew away from the Taipale River very fast and low, almost grazing the tree-tops. We thought the plane must have had Finnish markings on its wings. A couple of days earlier it had been announced that the Italian government had given our air force a few pursuit planes of that color as a gift. I don't know.

We tried to dig hollows into the sides of the trenches where a man could go to be safe and hidden from enemy eyes, although such pits could not withstand aerial bombs or a direct hit from the artillery. We began the digging with bayonets and finished it off with shovels, so that some of us had a nook like a barn-swallow's nest to go into. The boys searched for all kinds of junk, pieces of tent fabric and sacking to cover the mouths of those hollows, or used their own overcoats. We dug them while we were waiting. But of course there was no heating apparatus in such lodgings except for that from body warmth and smoking.

It was in the trenches at the Taipale River where I learned to smoke. I'd never had a cigarette in my mouth till then. I started smoking to pass the time away, and to heat the barn-swallow's nest that I dug into the side of a trench.

My kid brother took up smoking too. He was at the ripest age to start, but he didn't have the habit for long. For me smoking became a lifelong problem. I still haven't been able to quit though I've tried many times. Smoking stayed with me as a souvenir of the Winter War, along with a perpetual headache. I might have gotten the headache when I fell asleep in a trench at Vuosalmi in the last days of the war and my head froze fast to the ground. At least that's where I think I got it, since it started then and there. Ever since it has never let up for any length of time, even when I take so many headache pills that my stomach starts acting up. It was a strange awakening there at Vuosalmi, when they yelled that the Russians were on us. I tried to get up but couldn't get my head free from the ground. I didn't even understand at first what was wrong when I tried to jerk my head loose and get up. I thought an enemy bullet or piece of shrapnel had hit me while I slept and that I was paralyzed. I stayed stuck to the ground until the boys persuaded the Russians to turn back, that no one would get into our positions. Only then were they able to get my hair loose from the ground. Since there was no water they were at first going to piss on my head to melt the ice, but I said no, so they cut my hair with their hunting knives so I could get to my feet. But this didn't happen until the beginning of March when we were at Vuosalmi.

XVI

In the evening a cat meowed in front of our dugout. We took it in and the boys gave it some milk thawed from a frozen can. The cat was hungry. It ate everything they gave it and drank the milk. We thought it would become a real house cat for us there on the Taipale River, to keep us company and remind us that there was something more in the world than the Terenttilä field and the Russians attacking across it and the tank guns we had to keep firing on in fear for our lives, and the Russian artillery barrages.

The cat was in our dugout the entire night. Many of the boys went to stroke it. That set the animal to purring contentedly in the warmth with its belly full of food. We thought it enjoyed our company and would become the house cat in our dugout, but in the morning the cat wanted out and we never saw it again. They say a cat gets attached to places; if the people of the house move, the cat stays. A dog, though, goes with the people. A dog is humble, but a cat is proud. The cat that came into our dugout must have been from one of the Hiekkala houses or from farther away. It must have stayed at home when the people of the house were evacuated. It did not become attached to us, although the boys did their best.

Our company commander came to our dugout in the morning.

He asked those who had been on watch at night if they had heard anything unusual. The second lieutenant commanding a nearby unit had set out at night to look for papers on the bodies of dead Russians in order to see if more troops were coming on line opposite us. The man had not come back. We never found him even though we searched for him all the time we were at Taipale. He had disappeared completely.

When they set off for the war, our commander had promised the man's father he would sort of look after him — as much as he could. He was very unhappy when the man disappeared. He himself had gone out in front of the lines to look for the lost second lieutenant's body, but had not found it. Only during the second war when our troops had retaken Taipale and it was again Finnish territory did they find the body on the riverbank. They were able to identify it by its dogtags. The Russians had apparently taken him prisoner and killed him there. I don't know for sure.

The company commander also said that this was Stalin's birthday and maybe the Russians would want to give Father Stalin a birthday present by coming through our lines and destroying our positions. But nothing special happened.

We waited out the morning in the trenches for the Russians to prepare their birthday present for Stalin, but all that happened was that the artillery and aerial bombs kept grinding up the earth. Now and then a boy of ours was killed or wounded in honor of Stalin's birthday.

Only in the afternoon did the Russians resume their habit of assembling some ten tanks at the edge of the Terenttilä field with a platoon of men behind every tank, cutting loose with their artillery, and then starting across the field toward our positions. But we had learned all the required tasks, and we shot the infantry before they even got close to our positions. While the Russian infantrymen lay like brown bundles on the field at Terenttilä, the tanks drove up to the barriers before our positions and fired at us as if they were angry. Sitting in the nests dug into the sides of our trench, we let them vent their rage. Their fire went by us and we didn't try to do anything to the tanks. Having fumed and fired for a while, the tanks turned and drove out of the field and we had a breathing spell. Soon the Russian artillery began to fire on us again. It would have been a really monotonous war if we hadn't been so afraid and hadn't kept losing boys all the time. We were afraid too that the Russians would start doing something new, something they hadn't tried before, to which we couldn't react quickly. And we were always afraid of losing our positions and a lot of our boys.

In the afternoon when the attack was over, the regimental commander and Laurila came to our positions and checked the condition of our trenches along with our company commander. They ordered that men from the reserve battalion be sent to help us dig open the trenches again, since the fire of the Russian tanks and the artillery had filled them in badly during the day.

Laurila checked the field at Terenttilä and chatted with our company commander about how long the Russians would keep trying to cross the field in the same way by driving the tanks in an open line and ordering the infantrymen to run after them in the deep snow. Laurila said it could take a long time before the Russians started trying new tactics. The Russian army was big and had plenty of men, but a change in battle regulations took a long time in such an army. Nor did the Russian officers have the option of devising new methods of fighting since tactics were dictated by regulations, regulations which had been made for fighting on the steppes and in larger open areas than the field at Terenttilä. Laurila said that all we had to do was to stand and shoot them while they ran through the snow and hope that we weren't hit by a bullet or shell fragment.

He knew the ways of war and the ways of armies, this man who had fought in the German army. He knew our company commander well because both of them had been active in Civil Guard circles during the thirties and had trained the men from Ostrobothnia in the ways of war. Laurila had been at it as a commanding officer ever since the establishment of the Civil Guard. Everyone who knew him in those days called him Piiri-Matti.

There in our trenches they planned how the digging work was to be carried out and where to put the tank obstacles and barbed-wire mounts out in front of our positions to replace the ones shot up or crushed by tanks. They figured out where the anti-tank guns would do the most damage and the best way to kill Russians in the field at Terenttilä. As they did that I got a very clear and strong sense that these men knew what we were doing here. Deep down the rest of us always felt kind of scared and uncertain, but the calmness of those two made it easier for us. We could see that they were professionals and we knew it was always good to have professionals on a job no matter what it was.

It's the spit-and-polish ones who ruin everyone's morale. I got to see plenty of them too, especially during the second war when the officers were more fanatical. They tried in the German way to turn Finns into something they were never cut out to be, but they couldn't do it, no matter how hard they tried. The spirit of the Winter War was something different. These older Civil Guard officers were just doing what they had prepared themselves for and what they had trained their men for during all the years between the wars. They were doing it as well as they knew how and they were doing it calmly.

The company commander told Laurila about the second lieutenant from the nearby platoon who had disappeared at night, that his body had not been found. One could see that it depressed Laurila. He knew all these officers and most of the men. We saw that he grieved for every fallen man from Ostrobothnia. He didn't grieve for the Russians, at least he didn't show it. I don't know.

They behaved in a soldierly way in front of the soldiers and addressed each other formally, one of them a lieutenant colonel and the other only a lieutenant, although we knew they were close acquaintants and good friends and nearly the same age. Laurila was then a little over forty and our company commander was a couple of years younger. The infantrymen who had been trained in Germany had been elevated to high rank as young men. They became the army's officer cadre during the war of independence as well as after the war when the regular army was established. There were no other officers except for these infantrymen and those who came from the old Russian army.

As soon as Laurila had left for his command post or wherever he might be going to check other company positions, we were brought word that the Russians were moving through the Terenttilä swamp. We had to go and drive them back to keep them from flanking our lines and knifing us in the back.

When he got word of this, our company commander began planning with his platoon leader to drive out the Russians. We had been on so many wild goose chases caused by false alarms that the two officers wondered if there was anything important in the Terenttilä swamp. They decided that a platoon leader should take half a platoon and check to see if the enemy was really there.

The other half of the platoon would stay in our positions to keep watch on what the Russians were doing in the Terenttilä field and beyond it.

We circled around behind the lines toward the swamp, which was a juncture point for two regiments. The Russians had reached that point. The boys had not really decided whose task it was to drive the Russians back so no one had done it. They must not have been watching the juncture closely. There was a thin growth of dwarf pines in it, and the Russians were already halfway through the swamp when we reached its edge. They had one tank followed by infantrymen dragging small sled-like contraptions with machine guns mounted on them. They looked as if they were expecting the Finns to start shooting them since they knew they were not on their own land.

The platoon leader gave us a hand signal to form a skirmish line and pass on the word. He would fire first and then we were to open up with all our weapons. He had his own Guard rifle, an accurate one. He was a good shot and the leader of a Guard detachment. He preferred to fire his own rifle because he knew he would hit what he aimed at.

As soon as he fired, we began to bang away at the swamp, although I knew we'd have a tough time with the tank. The terrain was open and the tank crew would see at once where our skirmish line was. And we were lying only in pits in the snow. Snow won't stop a tank's fire.

It was a light, English-built tank, which we could have set fire to if we could have gotten close enough, but in the open swamp there was no chance of that. The tank returned our fire at once. We tried to shoot both the tank and the men behind it, but the bullets ricocheted off the sides of the tank and went whistling off over the swamp.

The infantrymen behind the tank dove into the snow as soon as the shooting began. They fired at us with everything they had while the tank blasted away with its cannon. Soon the tank crew realized that we had no anti-tank weapons with us and started driving forward, firing, with the infantry running after them. Things were looking tough for us. We all started hunting for a good tree to hide behind and thinking of some way to get back home alive. Just then the turret lid of the tank popped open. Two men jumped out and began running away across the swamp. The tank was left sitting there, silent.

When that happened, the infantrymen got up and ran too. We shot many of them. Now there was silence. We got up from the snow, wondering what had happened to make the Russians leave. It should have been our turn to run from them, their turn to cross the swamp with their tank and infantry and kill us.

We went over to the tank. It was completely sound. Inside it lay one man with a bullet hole between his eyes. He was an officer, the tank commander. Our platoon leader took the papers from his pocket. He told us that as the tank stood there firing, he had seen an open slit in its front where he thought he saw two eyes and part of a person's forehead. He had snapped off a shot through the slit with his accurate rifle. It hit the man between the eyes and killed him. That platoon leader was one good shot.

We went back to our positions and sent word to the Central Finland regiment that there were no enemy forces in the Terenttilä swamp now. To our own regiment we sent word that someone should go and drive the tank from the swamp to our own lines for use by the Finnish army. The tank was a sound and usable tool, if only its commander knew enough not to stare out at an enemy sharpshooter's rifle barrel through the tank's open peephole.

Now everything was quiet in our own positions. The Russians had organized no large attack at Terenttilä on Stalin's birthday. We hoped that they would celebrate the birthday in a more peaceable way, and in the evening we did begin to hear loud noises and whooping from their positions.

From time to time they fired away on the river bank and detonated charges in back of the Schoolhouse Woods. We guessed that liquor had been doled out to them, that under its influence they might still launch some kind of assault. But they made no further attacks that night. The racket and shouting went on till midnight. The boys insisted that they heard women's voices too, singing and shrieking, but we never did find out if they came from loudspeakers or if the Russian lads had women there. In any case, they were not planning the overthrow of the White Finns on that night.

We let the Russians celebrate. Around eight in the evening the battalion chaplain came and held a service at our platoon's dugout. We sang hymns and the preacher spoke and administered the Eucharist. We all partook of it, many of us on our knees. There wasn't room enough in the dugout for all of us to kneel, so many had to do it while standing. We sang hymns so loudly that the dugout rang. Our mood was devout. Everyone had the Lord on his mind. It was a place where a man, for all he knew, could be facing death.

XVII

At night the men on guard raised an alarm, but when we ran to our positions and peered out at the terrain before us, we saw not a single one of the enemy. We could hear them whooping from the direction of the river; they were still celebrating there. Or at least we thought so. We went to bed.

There was another alarm about four o'clock. One of the men on guard came in scared out of his wits. He swore that a whole company of Russians was attacking our positions, but when we ran to our posts, we did not see a single one of them in the field. From a couple of hundred yards away, in the direction of the next strong point, we heard a burst of firing, but even that did not last long. So we figured that the Russians had sent out a patrol to see if our watch was awake. Many of our boys were getting jittery from lack of sleep. The fear of death was always at the back of our minds. Many men had to be sent to the rear because their nerves went bad.

We really didn't get to sleep at all that night because of the alarms. My brother and I had the six-o'clock watch. We went to the guard post and tried to keep warm while peering at what was happening out in front of the line. Everything seemed to be quiet. At long intervals there was artillery fire somewhere off toward the Kirvesmäki positions. Then my brother insisted that he had heard some sounds out in front of us, from very close up. I tried to listen and I too heard something but I couldn't make out what it was. We wondered what could be so close up, only a few dozen meters from our positions. We tried going out to see without any luck.

It began to grow light. A tank came into the field from the Schoolhouse Woods, pulling a sled with some twenty Russians on it. They sat there whooping and waving as if they were going to a fair. We wondered what they were up to. My brother said we should use the machine gun at the watch post and shoot them all. They were within range. I said it would do us no good; they weren't attacking us but were out joy-riding. Let them go on with it as long as they wanted to. We could fire as soon as they turned the tank in our direction and started pulling the sleigh toward us.

They had already reached the middle of the clearing, seemingly with fun on their minds, and had turned around. At that moment our platoon leader came up. He said we should shoot the Russians on the sleigh. I said they were sure to answer with artillery fire if we started to annoy them with the machine gun, but the platoon leader said the Russians would start their barrage as soon as they sobered up whether we shot the men or not. He took the machine gun and started firing, killing them all. The Russians dropped from the sleigh like sacks thrown on a roadside. The tank did not slacken speed or change direction. By the time the tank made it to the edge of the clearing, there was not a single man left on the sleigh.

The artillery began to chew up our positions immediately and for a couple of hours we had to take shelter in our foxholes in fear for our lives. We could not leave the holes at all during the barrage.

The platoon leader crowded in next to me. We argued about whether they were firing because he had shot the Russians on the sleigh. The platoon leader insisted that the barrage would have come anyway because the Russians had begun one every morning. I didn't believe him.

From another foxhole we heard my brother yell above the noise of the explosions that he thought there were hand grenades mixed in with the artillery shells. We looked up too to see just what kind of metal was raining down on us. There were hand grenades flying into the trench.

The platoon leader rose in the midst of the shelling and the grenades and looked over the edge of the trench. He shouted that the Russians had dug themselves so close to our positions that they could throw hand grenades at us from their trench. We could not figure out when they had done the digging and why no one had noticed it. The platoon leader said they must have been digging for many nights, that they had raised a ruckus last night because the digging had come so close to our positions. I said we'd heard strange sounds but had not understood their source. Now we decided it was the Russians digging their trench.

The platoon leader was in a quandary about how to drive them away. We did not know how many were there only about twenty meters away, waiting for the artillery concentration to end so they could attack our pits. My brother and I stayed there on watch while the platoon leader ran through the exploding shells and hand grenades and brought the boys from the dugouts into their positions. We saw that we could not drive the Russians out with our artillery because their trench was too close to our positions, so the boys started heaving hand grenades and more powerful satchel charges over to the Russian side. All that morning we threw explosive stuff at one another. Then the hand grenades stopped coming from the Russian side. It wasn't until the night that we got to see what we had accomplished: the trench was full of dead Russians. The boys counted at least a hundred dead there.

In the evening the company commander visited our positions. He said the Russians had now adopted the tactic of digging right up to our positions and launching a surprise attack once they were near enough. They had done this with other companies as well, but not a single one of them had gotten into our positions.

He ordered the men on guard to be on the alert for sounds of digging. If any were heard they were to report to him at once so that he could order greetings for the Russians from the artillery. He stayed in our positions for a long time and talked about tomorrow being Christmas Eve. Packages from home had arrived, which he would distribute tomorrow. He ordered us all to be good so that Santa Claus would remember us. Then he left. That was the last time many of us saw him alive.

XVIII

Mybrother woke me up in the morning and said we would have to go and guard our country's shores. I've always been hard to wake up; it takes hours in the morning before I really grasp what is going on in the world. It's as if I were still asleep, would awaken for a little while, and then nod off again, although I do know all the time that I am awake here on earth.

It is a kind of borderland existence, especially if I have to go and walk somewhere right after rising, Then it's even harder to wake up. As I walk I feel as if I might be sleeping and sometimes I don't remember parts of the journey afterwards. When I get to the destination I wonder just how I got there and by what route. This Christmas morning, however, I woke up as soon as we came out of the dugout, for the Russian artillery concentration was massive. The whole earth seemed to be filled with the roar of their mortar and artillery shells.

My brother and I went crouching along the trench to our guard post, sometimes crawling right on our bellies along the ground. It had snowed during the night, and the bottom and the top edges of the trench were still covered with clean snow. We crawled humbly in that fresh, white snow toward our guard post. My brother was ahead, and I tried to call out to him to try to stay low and close to the ground. He was always inclined to stand up and walk straight ahead because it was hard for him to crawl and it looked so stupid. He was ashamed to crawl all the way to the guard foxhole. There were men we knew from our village there. My brother thought they would tease him about crawling. He didn't want them to think he was scared. He was still that much of a boy. I didn't have any shame in that regard. I crawled.

Before we reached the guard foxhole, I lost sight of my kid brother. His Lapland boots had disappeared around a corner. There was a loud explosion. I jumped up and ran to the spot. A mortar round had scored a direct hit on the trench. The shell had landed on my kid brother as he crawled on his belly along the bottom of the trench. It exploded there, killing him instantly. His entire midriff had been blown about the floor and sides of the trench. His legs and lower trunk, and his body from the chest on up were intact. At first I could do nothing. I wanted to put those pieces together, but I knew that so much was missing from the middle that the remaining pieces would not fit together. I knew I could not make a whole body of them. I dragged the upper body and the lower body separately toward the guard foxhole. One of the men on guard came to help me.

The other man on guard came out of his foxhole, saw what we were doing, and ran toward the dugout through the shell fire. He told us to keep an eye on Terenttilä for the time being. Soon a medic and the platoon leader and some other boys came from the dugout. The medic made no attempt to bandage my kid brother. I tried to pick up pieces of his midriff from the sides of the trench, the bigger ones, so they could go with the rest of his body into the earth of our home parish. I did not want his flesh to lie and rot in Taipale. Of course I couldn't get it all together, and there was blood everywhere. That is to be expected when a person takes a direct hit from a mortar shell.

We wrapped my brother's body in a piece of cloth. The platoon leader relieved me from my turn on guard duty and ordered someone else to take my place. I don't remember who it was. It didn't stick in my mind. I carried my kid brother to the front of the dugout and left him there. Or the bundle in which the pieces of his body were.

I went into the dugout. None of the boys could say anything to me. I sat down on the edge of a bunk, my brother's bunk, and thought that now the relations between the Russians and me were so shattered you couldn't find a sound spot in them. No matter how you tried to patch them. That's what they did when they cut my brother in half with a mortar shell.

It took a long time before I could think of a Russian calmly, without at the same time remembering our Paavo's body cut in half and the chopped meat of his midriff at the edge of that field at Terenttilä that Christmas Eve of thirty-nine. That's the kind of blow it was to me. Paavo was only twenty, and although Jussi was still younger when he got a bullet in his head on *The Isthmus* in forty-four, at least there was this difference: he was shot by our own infantry during the retreat. We were running toward home at Rajajoki and all our troops were so mixed up that we were ordered to attack a hill which was supposed to have a Russian emplacement. But it was our own infantry, and they too thought we were the enemy. They fired on us with all they had when we attacked the hill, and hit our Jussi. He was really only a child then, only eighteen. He was Mother's youngest so she loved him very much, but I was not able to save his life. He had been sent to Rajajoki at the very last minute, just before the start of the big

Russian offensive. He didn't have long to run around at the front. I tried in every way to protect him at Rajajoki and then on the flight through *The Isthmus*, at Kuuterselkä and in other tough spots. For Mother's sake I would almost have stepped in front of the bullet that hit Jussi if I could have seen it and gotten in its way in time. Paavo knew as much about the Taipale River war as I did, but no one can do anything about a direct hit from a mortar shell but the Father in Heaven, if that is His will.

Anyway, sitting there on the edge of Paavo's bunk, I came to think that this war had now become something personal with me. It was no longer between states and nations. The Russians had killed many boys I knew well, confirmation-school buddies and good friends from our village. To top it all they had now killed my brother, who in all good sense and reason should have had many years to live in this world, many joys before him. Sorrows too, of course. Now he would see none of them. That's what I thought then.

I gathered up Paavo's things to send home. There wasn't much. I took some of the clothes for myself, socks and a woolen shirt brought from home, which fit me since Paavo and I were about the same size, although he still had some of a boy's slimness.

As I gathered up Paavo's things and the boys sat there in the dugout watching in silence, the platoon leader ran in and shouted that the Russians were coming across the field in large numbers and everyone had to go quickly to his position. He said I could stay in the dugout if I felt too bad about my brother's death, but I promised to come to the trench as soon as I'd gathered up my brother's things. Somehow it seemed very important that his things be stored and in good order. I saw that he had saved all the letters he got from Mother and that girl while waiting for and during the war, the girl who had been leaning against him at the station when we were leaving. There were letters from still a third person. I separated the letters from his things to keep them from falling into the hands of outsiders or people who had no business with them and put them into my own pack. I didn't notice them there until the next week when we were already at the rest area in Putkinotko. I burned them one by one in the stove one night when it was my turn to be in charge of the fire. I thought at first that I wouldn't read them since they didn't belong to me, but I couldn't resist. There was nothing special in them.

The third letter-writer was a girl from Konnitsa, where we had waited for the war in November. Paavo had arranged to write to her. Her letters spoke only of the weather and of people I didn't know. Afterwards I thought that I shouldn't have burned the letters at Putkinotko. I should instead have brought them home with me when the war ended. It might have been nice to read them then.

While I was sitting there checking Paavo's things, the platoon leader ran into the dugout again and tried to call the company command post. But none of the telephone lines had withstood the pulverizing by the artillery which the Russians had sent us as a Christmas greeting that morning. So the platoon leader told me I should try to get to the company command post and tell the company commander that too many Russians were coming across the Terenttilä field, all headed for our position. They had lots of armor ahead of them. If the company had men available anywhere else they should be sent to our aid at once. He now had the feeling that we couldn't hold off this Russian attack with our own forces and would have to give up our positions. I promised to go.

I came out of our dugout and saw that the Russians were driving their tanks back and forth on the other side of the field.

There were large numbers of infantrymen behind the tanks. The artillery was still firing both on us and in back of us, so I had to pick my way carefully to avoid a hit from the big guns. I ran through a connecting trench and then through what was left of the woods. The company commander was in his command dugout. I told him what the platoon leader had ordered me to say: that the Russians were pouring toward this side of the Terenttilä field, not just a platoon or two, but at least a thousand men setting out from the opposite side.

The company commander was calm. He said he had already heard the same thing from other platoons and did not believe that all these enemy soldiers were driving toward our position alone. He believed they would test many positions at once, since that was their usual practice, according to Russian regulations.

The company commander promised to come quickly and see for himself what tack the Russians were taking today. He said I should tell the platoon leaders he would be there soon, that we should hold out till then. If it looked like we couldn't manage on our own, we would get more men from other platoons and from the battalion reserve if one existed. The artillery fire director was in the command post dugout too, and the company commander ordered him to call for artillery fire. The officer did make telephone contact with the battery and ordered it to fire in back of the Terenttilä field on coordinates already calculated.

I headed toward our own positions. The artillery was still covering them like a heavy blanket. Russian planes flew over dumping bombs, and pursuit planes flew back and forth strafing the trenches with machine guns. We had nothing to stop them with. I had to lie in the woods for a long time before I could get to the trenches. From there I saw our own artillery fire a strike in back of the Terenttilä field. It landed in the midst of the bunched-up tanks and Russian soldiers. They got so confused they started running for shelter. Finding none, they began running in circles in the field and on its fringe. The infantry running after the tanks looked like a kite's tail. I thought I saw many of their infantrymen killed by their own artillery fire and ground up by the treads of their own tanks. In their effort to flee, the tanks drove ruthlessly over the infantrymen. Three tanks caught fire. As they burned they sent plumes of black oil smoke into the cold, pale-blue sky.

At last I made it to our sector and told the platoon leader what our commander had ordered me to. He asked if I was ready to go to my position and take charge of it. I said yes, I would go. The platoon leader said that two more boys had been lost to the artillery fire. Six of them with shell fragments in all parts of their bodies had been sent to the first-aid station for bandaging. The line was now so thinly held that we would be hard pressed to stop the Russians if they got their forces together and started coming across the field in earnest.

And soon they came, their undamaged tanks lined up, followed by infantry armed with machine guns. The guns had a thick metal plate shielding them with the barrel protruding through a slot in it. And they were pushing a rapid-fire cannon on runners equipped with armor plate too, and there were lots of Russians, although many of them already lay dead on the field. Maybe they had brought additional forces from the river bank for the attack.

It was later reported that on this sector of the front from the mouth of the river to Terenttilä, the Russians had two divisions trying to break through. They always had almost twenty thousand men to a division, so that they had replacements enough for a few fallen men, maybe even for a few thousand.

Those Russians started coming across that field. When all that mass came rolling towards us we hoped that our artillery would fire again into the middle of the field. But no artillery fire came, and we had to start shooting Russians with every weapon we had, with machine guns and rifles and automatic rifles and machine pistols.

Our anti-tank guns succeeded in setting fire to two tanks that came right up to our position. That scared the other tanks. They drew back some distance and started firing their cannon at us. We shot the infantrymen when they came out from behind the tanks, shouting their spine-chilling attack shout as they came. It seemed to mean nothing, but came from deep within, from depths one could not believe possible in a human being. The Russians had even brought a rapid-fire cannon into their positions and were firing with that: shell bursts showered earth from the edges of our trenches and we kept losing men all the time, but not as many as the Russians, since we could lie in our positions in a shelter of sorts and they were under fire in the open with no protection but that afforded by the snow and shell holes.

By midday there was nothing they could do but try to get back to the banks of the Taipale River. It looked as if the officers and politruks were shooting their own men to keep them from running. But the officers could not contain such a mass of men. They ran once they had taken a notion to do so. They forgot all about us, just turned their backs and ran as fast as they could. Many of them died there.

The tanks turned back and drove noisily at high speed across the field, crushing the infantrymen with their treads. The officers and politruks shot them and we shot them. Many boys from the steppes reached their journey's end that day at Terenttilä. Afterwards we wondered if the men had been drunk when they

100

attacked. They must have fortified their courage with vodka. They came on with such stupid bravery, running upright and counting on their numbers. It made no sense to count on numbers when we were in trenches and could fire all our weapons calmly and accurately at those trying to get into them. It was a slaughter of human beings, that Christmas morning attack there at Terenttilä.

Only when the Russians had fled and we were sitting at the bottom of the trench trying to clean our weapons or getting cartridges from ammunition boxes or setting new potato-masher grenades within reach on the sides of the trench — it was only then that our platoon leader started to wonder what had happened to the company commander. He had known that we were facing a tough situation and had promised to come. We left boys on watch at our positions and went for dinner, or rather to eat. We knew that under such hammering by artillery no warm food could be made. Our lunch was mostly such that we got to chop off frozen pieces with our axes from a one-hundred kilo chunk of Swiss cheese and eat that with the hard bread.

When we came to the dugout we saw some strange movement behind it where a connecting trench joined ours. It was the company commander's messenger thrashing around, bleeding badly. The company commander was there too. He was dead, and so was the second messenger. They had been coming to our positions when a direct hit from a rapid-fire cannon had struck the company commander flush in the chest. He was badly mangled. Strangely enough, his head and face were untouched. He looked peaceful; you wouldn't have thought he was dead if you hadn't seen that there was only one shoulder and part of an arm joined to his head. His lower body was whole, but his chest and one arm were completely gone. The second messenger was still in one piece, but he was dead too. We fell silent, no one could say a word. The medic, a corporal, began bandaging the messenger who was still alive and two men set off for the aid station carrying him. He lived only until the following day.

We gathered up the pieces of the company commander and took them and the second messenger's body to the company command post for shipment home. The officers agreed among them that the leader of the second platoon would take over the duties of company commander and so notified the battalion. In the afternoon an adjutant from the battalion arrived to survey the situation. He saw how depressed we were by the company commander's death. The man had been like a father to us in the war and before that in the Guard, where he had been second in command. He was older than many of us and we had always trusted him completely. We agreed that we would never tell anyone at home how the direct hit had shattered him. Such things were not fit for the ears of people unaccustomed to war, especially women or children, or the company commander's family.

Potila, the adjutant, asked if we could hold off the Russians from our positions or if he had to start replacing us in the middle of the day. We'd taken large losses that day, our morale was low, and the Russians might come knocking again in the afternoon. But we all felt there was little they could do to us after all the deaths they had dealt us that day. We had lost so many men we knew. They had killed our company commander, mutilated him so badly. For my part, the Russians had taken my kid brother from me that morning. I had promised to protect him and look after him in the war. So we said to Potila that we were sure we could hold the position.

In the afternoon the Russians started a new war and they fought with us until nightfall, but these afternoon attacks lacked strength and authority. They did not even get close to our positions. They seemed to be suffering from a hangover. I don't know. But their artillery and mortar fire was pretty heavy and their airplanes harassed us the entire time and made us wonder where the Finnish air arm was hiding. They had been such big heroes before the war, doing all kinds of Immelman turns in stunt-flying demonstrations put on by the military aviation school. And all summer long they had been out shooting up swamps with live ammunition in their machine guns. Here we never saw them. The Russians could fly freely over us to their heart's content, sowing bombs and shooting up our positions with machine guns. Only when darkness fell that day did we have Christmas peace from the Russian infantry and armor, but the crunching of the artillery continued far into the night.

Christmas packages is what the boys called them then, the Russian heavy artillery shells that landed on the field throughout the night in front of our positions and behind them, where they exploded or lay unexploded. There were still a lot of duds among them. Why so many shells they fired were duds I don't know.

XIX

On Christmas Eve the packages and letters from home which the company commander had mentioned the evening before had been brought to our dugout, but many of the recipients were no longer here. They had been sent homeward in wounded transport or in coffins. We gathered their packages on an empty bunk and sent them back the next day with the horses and drivers that came to haul the bodies away. We felt that we had to take care of our buddies to the end. For example, we always tried to bring back the dead, even from no-man's-land, when boys died in counter-attacks or on combat patrols. And we lost many medics when they were dragging the boys back to our own lines and taking them to the aid stations.

On Christmas morning the boys said there was a pastor at the Central Finland regiment who had put on a regular army uniform and fought there as a platoon leader, a second lieutenant. They decided that we should have a Christmas service in our dugout too. Many of us had never spent a Christmas without going to a Christmas service. Even those who had not cared to go to church at home did not object when the boys left for the Central Finland unit's sector in the dim light of morning to hunt up the pastor.

The second lieutenant objected at first, saying that he was

fighting a war and had left the preacher at home, but the boys, having found him at last, would not let him off so easily. They brought him into our dugout early in the morning, about nine o'clock.

Only the men on watch stayed on line. All the rest of us tried to crowd into the dugout where the pastor held the service. The Russian artillery tossed shells outside the dugout and on the lines and into the woods in back of the lines. The pastor sometimes had to shout out his sermon to avoid being drowned out by the shell bursts. When the last hymn was being sung, Erkkilä kicked the door open and said: "Let the Russians hear how we sing hymns here."

The name of the pastor who was a second lieutenant with the Central Finland regiment at Taipale was Lehtinen. He was said to have been a fearless man there since his relationship to God was clear and unqualified. He later became our bishop when a bishopric was established at Lapua. After he came to Lapua he often recalled that Christmas service at Taipale and Erkkilä's going to kick the door open so that the Russians too could hear how the men from Ostrobothnia sang a Christmas hymn.

After the second lieutenant finished the Christmas service and left for his own unit, we got to sit in the dugout for another hour before the first alarm came and we again had to run to our foxholes to see what kind of Christmas program our neighbor had planned for us. We had to stand there until late in the afternoon. During that time, the Russians would come out into the field from the shelter of the Schoolhouse Woods, but they would always turn back into the woods and stay out of sight for a while. Then they would come to the field again, and bunch up as if they were about to attack. But they didn't attack, they went back into the woods.

There were many hundreds of men, and they had tanks for support. We could never tell which company's position they meant to attack. They came out to the field five or six times, but always went back into the woods. We were beginning to believe that their troops were getting rebellious, that the infantrymen were refusing to go out into the Terenttilä field to be killed. Life must have been dear to them too, that is, their own lives. Our artillery fired a strike into the Schoolhouse Woods, but we couldn't see if it did any good, the Russians were so well hidden by the woods. It was very cold. Whenever the Russians were out of sight I felt as if I were freezing and tried in every way to stay warm. But every time the tanks assembled at the edge of the woods and the infantry grouped for an attack, I became strangely warm. I remembered that afterwards.

In the afternoon the Russians drove their tanks into the field, with clusters of men running behind each tank. This time they did not stop at the edge of the woods but began moving toward our lines. Their tanks and infantrymen were split into groups before our positions so that no one point was the center of the attack. It was their way of finding the weakest point in the Terenttilä defensive line to come through. But there were no weak points in the line, at least not while our regiment was manning it. Our ranks were badly thinned since we had lost so many boys during those days, but we'd gotten replacements from the reserves. They were not known to us nor were they accustomed to fighting in this sector, but they had seen enough front-line action, and they learned quickly how to fight here. For death was their teacher. We soon saw that we could depend on them completely.

As the tanks and infantry advanced across the field to attack, the artillery increased its fire. There is no way to describe its power. In that fiery furnace we tried to peer over the edge of the foxholes until the foot soldiers had come within range of our fire. When they were close enough, we rose to the edge of the foxholes and began to return fire.

They did not break through this time either. They lay in the snow exposed to our fire and returning it with all their infantry weapons, while the tanks blasted us so hard with their cannon that earth spouted from the banks of the trenches. The tanks drove back and forth too, trying to smash the tank barriers and flatten the barbed-wire mounts.

We lost a lot of boys there too, but it was another day of horror and death for the Russians. Their infantry were left lying so close to us that we could throw hand grenades among them and our weapons could mow them down.

When two of the tanks had caught fire and the anti-tank men had hit another, the rest of them drew back a way. They thought they had run into our mine fields, although our engineers had been able to plant only a few mines that the tanks had now run into. When the tanks withdrew to fire at us from farther off in the clearing, the infantrymen were left lying exposed to our fire. We fought that whole afternoon and evening. We were able to get new forces from the reserve in place of the dead and dying, but our artillery and mortars saw to it that the Russians could not reinforce their unit, which now lay in front of our positions exposed to our fire.

The afternoon went by in that way. In the awful din of firing and shell bursts and explosions of aerial bombs, you felt drugged, as if time had ceased to exist. It was like coming from somewhere and being left behind; there seemed to be no future, only the here and now and the work we were doing — firing, loading, throwing hand grenades. And all the time the deafening roar of the weapons on both sides of the front.

At the end of the afternoon the Russians finally became convinced that they were not given leave to march this day from the Taipale River across the field at Terenttilä and on into Finland. Those still living withdrew, but that day they did not run off in a panic. They crawled humbly along the ground, firing at us all the way.

When the Russians were gone, two hundred and fifty of their boys lay dead, waiting to enter what we called the communist paradise. We didn't know what they thought paradise was like or if it was very different from ours. Six of our boys died that day and thirty were wounded. That Christmas day of thirty-nine at Terenttilä on the Taipale was not without cost for us either. For our company, I mean.

We were notified that there would be a change on the following night. The Central Finland regiment which had been in reserve would replace the Laurila regiment from Ostrobothnia on the sector where we'd had to fight since the middle of December. The news cheered us up a lot. We were tired and depressed by the deaths of so many friends during the last three days. I had lost my brother from a direct hit by a mortar shell. We had all felt the death of the company commander deeply. And we'd had little food and sleep all the time we had been on line.

The commander of the machine-gun company came later that evening to ask if we could wait until nighttime in our positions because switching in the dark would be safer. The battalion commander had ordered him to come to check our positions and to take over command in case our new company commander was not up to fighting and leading his men. As a platoon leader he'd had to go without sleep for many days before the death of the old company commander, going round to all the platoon positions and seeing to it that we always had Finns to throw in wherever the Russians tried to break through the lines.

We told him we could manage for one evening longer since we knew we would be relieved that night. We did not think that the Russians would start fighting in the dusk of evening, but as it happened, they gave us no peace to make the switch. Instead they kept up a constant artillery fire, and sent large units of infantry at our positions all night long. They tried hard to break through. We even had to fight hand-to-hand with them before they were convinced there would be no entry here.

The Russians kept it up all night, and on into the morning of St. Stephen's Day, not letting us close our eyes at all. We could not think of changing the units until the Russian pressure on our position had eased. Other companies had been able to switch earlier, but it was late in the evening of St. Stephen's Day before we got off the line. Actually it was already night.

XX

The exchange at the front line took place one man at a time, for the Russians were close to us all the time, keeping us alert and cautious. We had to lie on the bank of the foxhole and wait until our replacement came up to us, then point out the field of fire to him, the places from which the Russians had last fired on us, and explain a bit about lying in those nests in the sides of the trench during artillery fire and about staying warm.

In the Central Finland unit there were many inexperienced men who had joined the outfit while it was in a rest area, but there were also many who had been in the war from the beginning, who had fought the Russians in this same terrain and knew what this business of war was all about. The man who came to take my place did tell me his name, but I've forgotten it. It was some common name. When I started to explain this war business to him, he listened in a serious and matter-of-fact way. Then he told me he'd been afraid of the Russians already at the beginning of December.

When I had explained the layout to the man, I started along the trench leading to the company command dugout. The company was assembled there and we were led to the rear in darkness, leaving behind the field at Terenttilä and our defenses, which we had held for ten days, or more than that. From that field we had sent many coffins of boys we knew to our home parish. We had grown attached to the place and told the men from Central Finland what to do when the Russians tried to come through and take it again. We told them they must never give it up.

We marched five or six kilometers back from the front lines to a place called Putkinotko, a river, or a brook channel, where the engineers had built a dugout village our whole battalion fit into.

It felt as if I had slept for many days, but thinking about it afterward, I also did all kinds of things that I was unaware of in my sleepy daze: I went to the sauna and changed into clean clothes.

Replacements arrived, bringing our company nearly to full strength, a couple of hundred men. When we left Terenttilä, a count taken at the company commander's orders had come to sixty-seven men. The replacements were mostly from our home area, but a few men from other provinces had strayed into the group.

I remember getting a letter from home while at Putkinotko and I must have written home from there, since my wife has the letters in her keeping. She has every letter I wrote during that first war and during the second one too. I have never written any other letters home. I've sometimes read those letters, after the war.

We were allowed to rest and sleep a few days at Putkinotko. We took saunas in the evening and at night, and during the day we lay about in the dugouts. All the boys were so tired and dazed by the fighting that some of them didn't really begin to function until New Year's Eve. In one of the dugouts the boys observed Christmas and New Year at the same time because during the Taipale fighting they'd not been able even to think about celebrating Christmas.

After New Year's they had us start making fortifications at night, since it was impossible to make them during the day on account of the Russian planes. So we had to give up our night-time saunas.

We built a defense line farther back in case the Russians broke through the Central Finlanders' defenses and forced them to withdraw from Terenttilä and the mouth of the Taipale River. We also made barbed-wire mounts which were taken by the hundreds to the Terenttilä swamp, for trees grew there so sparsely that we could not mount barbed-wire barriers on them. There was also talk of building tank obstacles at the rear defenses, but we considered them useless. We had seen that the Russian tanks were no big problem. Their appearance was more scary than what they could do. The boys had set them on fire with burning bottles, those Molotov cocktails, they had been shot into scrap iron by the artillery on the field at Terenttilä, and our platoon leader had put one of them out of commission by shooting the tank commander between the eyes. So we came to the conclusion that we weren't going to waste our time building tank obstructions since they could be stopped in other ways. The tanks had not really tried to drive through our lines, but had been content to belch at us with their guns, and no obstacles could prevent that. So we merely dug pits in front of these rear defense lines, deep pits over which the tanks could not drive, into which they would fall if they tried to come through.

Before the end of the year, we had a big scare. News arrived that the Russians were planning a big attack on Kirvesmäki in Koukkuniemi. Men from Central Finland were there too, protecting their country. It was feared that there was no way they could stop the overwhelming number of Russians which reconnaissance had discovered and which prisoners had told us about. In the afternoon on the thirtieth of December we were put on an alert for departure.

We got our weapons ready and sat in the dugout, afraid and waiting for the order to move out. Word would come from the regimental command post to the battalion and from the battalion directly to us whenever the men from Central Finland were forced to give ground. At times we went out of the dugout and listened to the roar of the battle from the direction of Kirvesmäki. From the sounds we could tell that things were tough there.

But they did not let the Russians through.

While we sat and waited to go and counterattack any positions taken at Kirvesmäki, a writer named Kalle Väänänen came and tried to entertain us with all kinds of funny stories in the Savo dialect. He went dutifully to all the dugouts, presenting his program and trying to perk up our spirits. They say he wrote many books in the Savo dialect, but we were sober-faced and didn't laugh. We weren't a good audience. Maybe that's where people get the idea that the men of Ostrobthnia are a humorless and sober lot who don't understand stories in the Savo dialect. At about five in the afternoon the alert was called off and we received word that the men of Central Finland had repulsed the big Russian attack and driven the Russians back to the bank of the Taipale River and that the positions at Kirvesmäki were in Finnish hands. Afterwards they said that the Russians had come right into the Finnish positions, but had been beaten back in a counterattack. A lot of the boys were lost there. At the time there were boys in the Central Finland regiment from Soini and Lehtimäki — that's the way the area was divided then — and their losses had been very heavy. The Russians had lost so many that when our troops got back into their own positions with a counterattack at the end of the afternoon there was so much blood in the trenches it came halfway up their boot-tops and in that blood the bodies of our own and the neighbor's boys had been swimming. In cleaning out the trenches, many of the men, even those with strong stomachs, threw up whatever they'd managed to eat that day. That's what they told us.

After the New Year, our rest period became a matter of doing field work evenings and nights and lying in the dugouts by day. When we came home at night we took a sauna. We didn't have much in the way of entertainment. Radio commentator Pekka Tiilikainen and editor Sulo Kolkka came to interview our battalion's boys about this Taipale miracle, but I wasn't in the bunch that was interviewed. I did get to see Tiilikainen up close; he was a lot thinner then than he was later as a radio sports commentator. They went around among the front-line troops and did interviews and the boys told about their heroic deeds and their feelings so that the people at home would believe that our enemy was not about to bury us. We had been away from the Terenttilä field long enough so that the boys' statements about the abilities of the Finnish soldier and the Finnish army were cocky and self-confident.

The confidence in Finnish soldiers was strong on the home front too in those days. One of our boys came to Putkinotko from home, where he had been on a convalescent leave. As soon as we came to the Taipale River in December he had taken shell fragments in his back and legs and been allowed to go and heal those wounds. He said that they swore as absolute fact that our platoon leader on the very first day at the Taipale River had killed thirty Russians with his hunting knife. When he had tried to argue and told them that he at least had never heard of any such killings, the villagers had gotten really mad and insisted that they had absolutely reliable information about it. So, at home, faith in the front-line troops was really firm.

Every day we expected to be sent back to the Taipale River. We were afraid that we would not get the ten days of rest promised us, that the ranks of the men from Central Finland would thin out so much that we would be thrown into the fire before the ten days agreed on were over.

Winter came in earnest, very cold and with so much snow that the drivers had to strain their horses to the limit. There were alerts on many days, and we sat in the dugouts ready to go, but we did not have to counterattack once. The men from Central Finland held the line.

It was not until the evening of the sixth of January that we left, and by then we had been back of the lines for ten days. Another year had arrived during that time. On leaving we got the news that we would relieve the men from Central Finland at the Taipale. When we got there we saw that the battalion would now occupy the Joensuu sector, which extended from the mouth of the Taipale River on the shore of Lake Ladoga to the mouth of the Kaarna River at the edge of the Terenttilä field. There the boys of the 19th infantry regiment, the third battalion, had been holding their own. The lines there ran almost from the bank of the Taipale River, where it leaves Lake Ladoga. The enemy was on the opposite bank of the river at a place called Kalatuvat. Our positions looked far out toward Terenttilä and the Pärssinen and the Schoolhouse Woods. Those places were familiar to us, but you couldn't call them dear.

The landscape had changed radically since we left it that St. Stephen's evening. You didn't recognize it at first. The earth had been ground black by the artillery and the trees were all down. Only long stumps were left standing. We saw all this on the morning of January seventh when daylight came. The men from Central Finland had really had a rough time of it.

XXI

Our first days on the Joensuu sector were quite peaceful. The very first day things were quiet on the whole Taipale front. In the afternoon we saw some fires in back of Neosaari on the other side of the Taipale River where the Russians were, but we couldn't find out what they were doing or if the fire was accidental or deliberate. We had a mixup ourselves: the engineers' maps of the mine fields didn't seem accurate because they had been made in the dark, and there was a danger that some of us might wander into our own mine fields. An officer of the engineers who had been directing the laying of the mine fields arrived later in the afternoon and made new maps which showed where the mines and the booby traps had been hidden.

In the evening they began to gather men for a patrol. I didn't happen to be chosen but got to stay at the base that night. My turn for watch duty came up in the morning, when the patrol came back. They said they had gone far out onto the ice of Ladoga on the enemy side but they had seen no enemy positions and not a single Vanya. They hadn't been able to take any prisoners, which had been one of the patrol's tasks, and had come home empty-handed.

I don't know if they had even gone to the other side of the Taipale River. They all swore they had crossed the river by circling the thawed spot at its mouth on the lake side, where the ice was thick and would bear their weight, then gone along the Ladoga shore in the direction of Leningrad, but had seen no Russians or any installations. Our gang doubted their story; we believed that they had crouched out in front of our own lines all night. The Russians, after all, were still fighting against us in this war. They hadn't gone home yet and taken their instruments of war with them.

Our own watch had seen a Russian patrol moving at the mouth of the Kaarna, where they had run into the engineers' mines. The Russians were believed to have lost many men to exploding mines. All day long men kept asking who would go to the mine fields the following night to find out what the Russians were doing at the mouth of the Kaarna River, which was no-man's-land. The Kaarna had carved a deep channel where it flows into the Taipale.

The next day was quite peaceful again. In the morning we saw the Russians planning something again, since there was a lot of movement in the Schoolhouse and Pärssinen Woods, and the artillery fire director, who was with us in our position, was calculating his coordinates to find out where it would be good to let fly with the big guns if the Russians really meant to hold a meeting there.

In the afternoon we began to hear a dog barking in back of Kalatuvat on the Russian side. The boys said it was always a sign that the Russians were sending messages to each other. It was their way: their communication equipment was so poor that they couldn't get it to work in such cold weather. It was then already forty below. The lowest reading at Taipale, I heard, was forty-nine below, but I don't know if it was an accurate reading.

We tried to figure out from the barking what message the Russians were sending to each other. We counted how many times the barking sounded and how long the interval always was between the barking. We also informed the battalion that this type of activity had been noted at Kalatuvat on the other side of the Taipale river, but that we were unable to solve the riddle of what that barking communicated since we did not know what secret language the Russians were using. We asked that some decoder of secret languages higher up interpret it.

Later in the evening we got word from the battalion command post that the fifth company's boys had also heard the barking from beyond Kalatuvat. Being better able to see the other side of the river from their positions, they were able to affirm that this time it was a real dog. They had seen it.

In the evening the company commander came to our dugout and asked for some men to go with him to the mouth of the Kaarna River to see what the Russians had been up to the night before. He wanted to see if there were papers left on the dead from which the headquarters could get an idea of Russian plans and objectives. Five of us went with him. The moon was bright and we could see well to walk. The company commander walked in the lead — that was always his way. He died in the Continuation War, a shell from a direct-trajectory cannon broke his thigh and we couldn't get him to care right away because we were nearly surrounded. The Russians were in front of us and there was a field behind us on which the enemy could fire with all his weapons. We were on a kind of a wooded island or point, and could not get the company commander out before he had lost too much blood. He asked the medics there on that wooded point how long the wound would take to heal, and when the medical sergeant told him it would surely take months before the large bone break would heal and his blood be okay, the company commander refused to believe him. He said he didn't have time to lie in bed so long when the war had just begun. He did not want to be out of the war for two months. That night he was dead.

At the mouth of the Kaarna River, he walked ahead of us; we had a strange and forsaken feeling because it was so light. The enemy could be somewhere watching us at the river mouth. He could lie in wait and shoot us all. When we reached the river channel we began to feel a little more secure, as if we had gotten into the shelter of walls.

The company commander had a map of the mine fields with him, and we circled them, being on guard for other mines too. For all we knew our neighbor had been laying mines in the river channel too. But we didn't run into any Russian mine fields there. At the mouth of the river we saw that a few of our mines had exploded, but we did not see any Russian bodies. Maybe they had carried the bodies back to their own side or then maybe none of their patrols had been there. I don't know. We returned the same way we had come to the river mouth and went to bed when we got back to the dugout.

The third day was peaceful too, the ninth day of January. Battalion had sent a patrol in back of the lines at the mouth of the Taipale River and that patrol had found the enemy on the other side of the river. In the afternoon we began to get more information when the boys visited the positions of other companies. Another patrol had run into the Russians on the shores of Ladoga and exchanged fire with them at night, but they hadn't taken any prisoners. They had come running back to their own side when the patrol leader had started firing at the Russian watch detachment with his machine pistol and our neighbor's men had started pouring out of the Russian dugouts. We couldn't help but wonder now which patrol's information was true and correct, the one which had not found the enemy on the shore of Ladoga or the other which claimed even to have been in a fire fight with them. Mostly the boys believed the latter patrol's account.

In the evening we heard the din of battle from Terenttilä, but could not see what was happening there. We could only hear that the boys were in a hard battle there with our neighbor's men. The first battalion of our regiment was defending the positions there.

We too were put on alert and waited until after midnight to see if the Russians would start coming toward our positions, but they did not make an attack on us.

It was not easy for them to attack in this direction, toward Linnankangas. We had the Kaarna River channel between us, and across it there was open ground and on this side in front of our position there was open ground, and two emplacements, the Woods emplacement and the Meadow emplacement, from which it would be easy to rake an attacker with machine-gun fire.

XXII

On morning of the tenth, the Russians again began to pound us with their artillery and mortars, laying down concentrations on the emplacements. They were not built to withstand such fire. A half-platoon from a machine-gun company was in the Meadow emplacement to keep an eye on the Russians and repel them if they started to attack. They had to abandon the emplacement; the heavy artillery fire was about to block its entrance completely and trap them in that coop. They got out by running across the meadow and through the woods to Pihkahovi in the midst of an artillery concentration. Only when they got there did they announce that the Meadow emplacement had been abandoned.

They were ordered to go back after dark to re-take the emplacement and reinforce it with sand bags to better withstand the pounding of the artillery. The emplacement was of poured concrete and there must have been some iron in it too, but it wasn't built for a modern war. While the lighter mortar and artillery shells burst harmlessly on it, a direct hit from a heavy shell would have destroyed it. The boys were afraid one would drop on their necks while they sat in it and smaller grenades kept exploding on the roof of the concrete cubby hole making a nasty noise, and we had all seen the tracks an aerial bomb leaves when it explodes, a crater ten meters in diameter and many meters deep. While waiting to be sent to the front lines in early December, we'd built a dugout shelter for a half-platoon in such a bomb crater. The Meadow emplacement could not have withstood a hit from a bomb like that.

On that day too, the Russians did no more than keep us alert with their artillery fire. They did not try to attack. Later we learned they had brought completely new, fresh divisions to the Taipale River front during these early January days. They'd had no time to attack while changing the troops.

A conviction spread among us that the Russians had had enough of breakthrough attempts, that they couldn't stand the heavy losses we knew they had suffered on our sector and on the eastern Isthmus. At Summa and Lähde hundreds of their tanks had been destroyed and they had lost men by the tens of thousands. And farther north there had been the big pincers movements at Raate and Suomussalmi — all this led our boys to believe that the Russians were running out of men and materiel. I didn't believe anything of the sort. Many others in our company doubted it too. Things were strangely calm those days, but we remembered only too well the strength and doggedness with which our neighbor had tried to break through our positions at Terenttilä, how they had harried the Central Finland regiment at Koukkuniemi and Kelja on the shores of the Suvanto.

From our positions we could clearly see the location of Russian mortars firing on us and on the Meadow and Woods emplacements. We sent the coordinates to our artillery, which really battered them. That silenced the mortar fire from Neosaari, and we had a respite for the rest of the afternoon. The Russian heavy artillery was firing, but on Terenttilä and Kirvesmäki, not on us.

We had time to watch the doings of our neighbor boys. There was a lot of movement around Neosaari. In the middle of the day, they worked at hauling away the wrecked trucks our artillery had earlier put out of commission near the Taipale ferry landing. We could see them hitching ropes and cables to the junked trucks, but as they towed them from the clearing, we could not see the tow trucks at all, only the junked trucks gliding one by one into the shelter of the woods. We asked our artillery to fire on them, since they were a good, clear target, but they refused. They were too low on ammunition to waste it on already disabled trucks and a few Vanyas. As far as they were concerned, the Russians could keep their wrecked trucks and other shot-up war materiel. The towing was another sign that the Russians were replacing their troops. Those who were leaving were taking their equipment with them.

All night long we could hear loud sounds from Neosaari and from beyond Kalatuvat all the way to the banks of the Taipale River: shouting, the driving of vehicles, and the clanking of tank treads. That kept us alert. We couldn't help hearing the sounds, but we had no idea what the Russians had in mind. We didn't know then that their divisions were being replaced.

Some claimed that the Russians were withdrawing their troops to the old border, since it was more honorable to start making peace when one's troops were within one's own borders. They could not then be accused of banditry and robbery of other people's land. But even then many of us believed that the Russians would not lightly give up the lands they had taken. Their losses had been too heavy. It was a question of a large country's prestige. Many of us felt that the Russians were only taking a breather and would soon start the game again. And that's what happened.

In the evening the engineers went through our positions to the mouth of the Kaarna River where some of their mines had exploded and reset the mine fields. On the way back they sat in our dugout for a while. They were from Kortesjärvi. We argued with them about whether a huge explosion we'd heard at Neosaari in the afternoon might have resulted from a direct hit on a Russian ammunition dump or explosives center. The engineers hadn't heard the explosion, but they believed that a Russian tank had run onto one of the anti-tank mines they had set. They had hidden the mines at Neosaari early in December. We argued about it back and forth. The men from Kortesjärvi declared that they knew everything about the sounds of explosives and tank mines going off. Our boys argued that they knew something about such matters too.

At night our neighbor began to plow the Neosaari road without trying to hide their work from us at all. They drove their trucks back and forth along the road with headlights blazing, opening up a wide furrow from somewhere in the vicinity of Rautu and Metsäpirtti to Neosaari and from there over the ice almost to the front lines.

I was at a listening post with Erkkilä. During the day he had been inclined to believe that the Russians were withdrawing across the old border, but the night-time plowing made him waver. He still tried to insist that it would be easier for them to transport men and equipment to new lines in back of Metsäpirtti along a plowed road, but he himself could no longer really believe it. We became convinced that we still had many trying days ahead of us with those neighbor's boys there at the Taipale River.

On the next day they opened up with a rapid-fire artillery piece, but our own artillery got it quieted. In the evening the men from the Meadow emplacement came, saying that its floor was now under thirty centimeters of water. Their felt boot-tops didn't exactly keep it out, although they were high enough. Men of the regiment's engineers came through our positions late in the evening to check out the emplacement.

When they returned after a long stay, they said the emplacement had to be left empty until the water froze sufficiently to use the ice as a floor. They could come up with no other solution. In their opinion, pumping would not keep it dry.

The machine-gun company was forced to take its men out of the Meadow emplacement. Our company was ordered to set up a listening post there at night to stop the Russians from coming and taking possession of it. It was considered a vital part of our defensive set-up.

XXIII

At night the Russians came up along the Kaarna River channel and attacked the Meadow emplacement. The men at our company's listening post there, three of them, ran off when the Russian attack began, thinking there was a large troop coming.

There were only about ten Russians however. They went into the emplacement and took possession of it. That turned out to be a lot of trouble for us, a real sore spot, for the Russians kept trying to bring more men from the Kaarna River channel to the emplacement. They began at once to dig a connecting trench toward the Kaarna River and another toward the Woods emplacement. They wanted to take that from us too so they could freely fire on our positions from it.

The three men from the emplacement had been forced to run toward the first battalion's positions. They hadn't dared cross the open space in front of ours. It wasn't until the next morning that they came over from the first battalion by circling through the swamp. They were still all spooked, saying that they had run into a Russian patrol behind our lines in the swamp. We didn't really know if we should put any stock in what they said, but we did send a patrol of our own to check if there were any Russians in the swamp and to drive them out if there were. And the Russian artillery began firing on us the first thing in the morning.

Our patrol found no enemy in the swamp. After they returned during the day, the three men from the emplacement were sent to the regiment for closer interrogation. They reported that they had run away from the Meadow emplacement because the Russians had been yelling so loudly and firing so heavily they thought a large troop was attacking them. There were only the three of them on guard. They had not fired a shot, but had run in the dark all the way to the neighboring battalion.

The men at another of our listening posts between our lines and the mouth of the Kaarna River had been scared by the Russian shouting and firing, but they had at least been able to run to their own company's positions.

Thus the entire bank of the Kaarna River and the Meadow emplacement were now in the hands of the Russians. They were hurriedly digging positions around the Meadow emplacement and connecting trenches toward the banks of the Kaarna River and toward the Woods emplacement. It was getting to the point where even battalion headquarters and the regimental commander were concerned.

We got an order from the regiment to take the Meadow emplacement from the Russians. The sixth company's boys set out to do it. But they did not take it. The Russians went into the emplacement, and when the boys tried to cross the clearing to get to it, the Russians fired at them. They had to come back and think of a better way to do the job.

Everyone was beginning to panic at the thought that the Russians were in the emplacement. They were afraid that more of them could cross to the north bank of the Kaarna River at any time and take all our positions. We got word that the artillery would fire a strike. We were ordered to attack immediately afterwards in company strength and drive back the Russians who were on the north bank of the river. But we didn't see any of them there although the visibility from our positions was good. We sent word that there were no Russians in front of our positions, but the battalion had other information. They actually had to come themselves and check before they would believe us.

We decided that it didn't pay to try to take the Meadow emplacement during the day. But we were ordered to stop any more Russians from getting to it.

It was morning already, and now the Russians tried to come to the aid of their comrades in the Meadow emplacement. They came into the clearing from the Pärssinen woods and attacked toward the first battalion positions. Many more began coming up from the banks of the Taipale River, trying to get into the Kaarna River channel and from there to the emplacement.

The Woods emplacement had no direct line of fire to them, but we could reach them from our own positions. Our artillery was also firing on them, cutting them off from the Kaarna River channel. They had to turn and try to get back to the bank of the Taipale River. We shot a lot of them there. Later I heard that the firing slit of the Woods emplacement had been blocked by the explosion of a mortar shell so our boys couldn't fire from there. In the afternoon a shell from the heavy artillery scored a direct hit on the Woods emplacement and blew it apart. We lost many of our boys there.

In the evening the boys of the fifth company attacked the Meadow emplacement as soon as it was dark and tried to take it, but they were forced back to our positions. The Russians kept up a heavy fire from the emplacement and their mortar shells were landing around it all the time. The Russians knew their men were safe inside it.

We had to stand in our positions that night and make sure that no more Russians came to the Meadow emplacement, firing flare pistols to keep the terrain before us lighted up. However, the Russians did not try to send more men to the Meadow casement, so actually we stayed awake the whole night for nothing. But we couldn't know that ahead of time.

It wasn't until the following day that the Russians came. In the morning we began to hear the sounds of men being assembled in large numbers at Neosaari. They crossed the Taipale River farther off in the vicinity of the Schoolhouse Woods or somewhere beyond, and moved in the shelter of the river bank to the mouth of the Kaarna River. We did not see them until they were running along the river channel up to the Meadow emplacement, which we had planned to take at about five or six as soon as it started getting dark. But now the Vanyas had sneaked up to it in order to help their comrades. Our plans and those of the Russians just didn't jibe at all.

Anyway the fifth company boys attacked the Meadow emplacement right after five and got the terrain under their control. But there were now lots of Russians on the ground beyond it to as far as the river bank, so the boys had to go on attacking. They bypassed the Russians in the emplacement and drove the others ahead of them along the Kaarna River channel towards the Taipale River. On the river bank the Russians took cover behind our tank barriers and directed a nasty fire at our boys from there. Many of the fifth company boys fell, including the company commander. They were nearly in hand-to-hand combat with the Russians, before drawing back. Then they kept throwing hand grenades at them for many hours. The Russians fired from behind the tank barriers and their mortars chewed up the Kaarna River channel and its banks. It wasn't until evening that they retreated, running across the field to the Schoolhouse Woods — that is, those who could still run.

Our neighbor's boys in the emplacement had shoveled earth over the firing slit on the inside and were sitting there waiting for someone to get them. We stationed boys to wait at the entrance in the same pits the Russians had managed to dig around the emplacement during the day.

During the day barbed-wire mounts which the reserve battalion had had time to make had been brought into our positions. We blocked the entire Kaarna River channel with them, so that the Russians could no longer come in its shelter to the aid of their comrades in the Meadow emplacement. The engineers set trip-wire mines along the channel. We were so busy the whole night, that we got very little sleep.

XXIV

After midnight the Russians tried to get to the Meadow emplacement. We heard them trading fire with the boys near it and with
the first battalion boys in the Terenttilä positions. They tried to
cross the field from the Pärssinen woods, which was a bad thing
to do even at night, for the field could be lighted up with flare
pistols. They couldn't make it to the emplacement.

In the morning we were ordered to help the men near the
emplacement. When we arrived we saw that the Russians were
still inside, with the boys from the fifth company around it in the
trenches dug by the Russians the day before. We started improving
the trenches and digging them deeper. The Russian artillery was
firing the whole time, making our digging awkward and difficult,
for we had to try to stay out of the artillery fire. We got the
trenches somewhat deeper and piled sandbags to brace their sides.

The boys of the fifth company were exhausted. They had been
awake for more than twenty-four hours, first in the attack on the
Meadow emplacement and then on the move to the Kaarna River
channel. After that they'd had to keep watch on the Russians
inside the emplacement day and night, and then they'd had to
counter the attack from the Pärssinen woods. They were disheart-
ened and gloomy. We tried to get their trenches into better shape.

At noon we went back to our own positions to get a bite to eat. The Russian artillery was grinding at us constantly as we sat in our dugout and tried to get some food down. Our company commander came in and asked about the situation at the emplacement. The whole regiment was concerned about it, and battalion kept asking for the latest information. The company commander told me a message had to be delivered to a fifth-company platoon leader near the Meadow emplacement, that I had to take it to him at once. I started wondering what information was so vital now that a person had to go into that artillery fire. I said we should wait a while for the fire to slack off, but the company commander repeated that I must go at once. I asked him why the message was so important, but he lost his temper and told me that was none of my business, that I was to do as I was ordered. Then when I asked him what his orders were, what my urgent message was, he told me to just go and say "hello" to the platoon leader. I asked if there was any other message. When there was no answer, I started off. Everyone's nerves were on edge because of the Meadow emplacement business and I left the dugout angrily, a piece of hard bread in my hand.

As I came out of the dugout I saw that the Russian artillery concentration was right on our position, but I was too stubborn to go back inside. I went on into the woods in back of our positions and through it toward the Meadow emplacement. Now out from under the artillery fire, I continued on through the woods. I could hear how badly the Russian artillery was pounding the Meadow emplacement and ran over in my mind the best way to reach it.

I came to a small clearing. A squad of our boys had a big campfire burning there and were warming themselves at it. They asked me for the password. I told them it was best to douse the fire quickly because it must already have been spotted by a

Russian airplane and they would soon be fired on by artillery. They argued that a person could not stay alive in these woods without a fire, that there was no other way to keep warm. They were anti-aircraft men, and they had a small anti-aircraft gun with which they were supposed to fire at Russian planes. I couldn't stop to argue, and went on toward the Meadow casement. I thought they would warm up fast enough when a Russian plane called for artillery fire on them. On the way back in the afternoon I saw that the Russians had fired a strike on them. The ack-ack gun lay twisted by the fire and all the men were dead, five men and a squad leader. I reported it so that they could take the bodies away. It bothered me — should I have kicked the fire to put it out and driven the boys away from the middle of the clearing? I don't know.

When I reached the men near the Meadow emplacement, I relayed my company commander's hello to the platoon leader. It puzzled him a bit, but at that moment the Russian artillery began laying down a heavy concentration which succeeded in blowing a hole in the emplacement wall. Three Russians came out through the hole and began running toward the Kaarna River channel and their own lines. The boys of the fifth company began firing at them, and the company commander had no further time to wonder at my hello. The boys shot two of the Russians, but the third ran so skillfully and luckily that he made it to safety into the Pärssinen woods, although thirty men were firing all kinds of weapons at him. When he had disappeared into the woods, the men opined that he deserved to be saved. Back at our company's position I reported the dead ack-ack men I had seen. Soon we were ordered back to the Meadow emplacement to dig trenches there the whole day under Russian artillery fire. At the end of the afternoon, around five, the company commander's messenger arrived with an order to return to our own positions and leave the Meadow emplacement to the fifth company boys. They did not want us to go. Their second lieutenant actually ordered us not to leave, but we had clear orders from our own company commander, so we left.

When we got to our own positions, the battalion commander along with his adjutant and other strangers was there in the trench with our company commander. They were all peering out toward the Kaarna River channel. A call had come from the Meadow emplacement after we left with the news that the Russians were now on the north bank of the river. There were said to be many of them and they were attacking near the emplacement.

We already had a listening post set up there and other men watching and lying in wait for the Russians. The battalion commander concluded that the men on watch near the Meadow emplacement were seeing things and thought our own men were the enemy.

Our platoon leader went to the mouth of the Kaarna River. On his return he said that all was quiet, that the men were in position at the listening post and had not seen a single Russian, which is why he had concluded that the group near the Meadow emplacement were so tired that they were seeing the enemy everywhere. He ordered our company to post some twenty men near the emplacement for the night to reinforce the fifth-company boys.

The company commander himself chose the men who would have to go to the Meadow emplacement for the night. We couldn't really scrape up twenty men, so in the end only fourteen of us went circling through the woods in back of us toward the Meadow emplacement.

It was a very dark night, cloudy and milder, and the temperature was said to be only about ten degrees. When we got close to the emplacement, the men there began firing at us with machine pistols and rifles. The leader of our detachment shouted the first part of the password, which was Bolshie-Devil, but no matter how much he shouted, they kept right on firing. Two of our boys were wounded, but no one was killed. We tried shouting to ask if there were any Finns there, but the answer we got was rifle fire. So we believed that the Russians had again taken possession of the ground and that our men had fled from there.

We came back to our own position, wondering what to do about the situation. We notified the battalion that our men would be fired on if they tried to approach the emplacement.

Battalion sent a patrol to the Meadow emplacement to find out if it was totally in control of the enemy. They came back soon and told us that the emplacement area was in our hands, but since the men there had not received word that our bunch was coming to help them, they had thought we were foreigners and had begun firing at us. They were so tired and spooked that they had taken the password for a foreign password. I just don't know. Two of our boys had been wounded, and it had been no great fun for any of us to be lying under that fire. Later our company commander sent a written clarification of the matter to the battalion commander which made it plain to everyone that this accident, the shooting at our own men, had resulted from the fifth-company boys' jitters. We had approached the Meadow emplacement the way we always had, which was the only safe and direct way to it. According to the boys of the fifth company, we had approached from the direction from which the Russians had attacked a little earlier. They insisted that only Russians had come that way before.

That night our bosses decided to stop the squabbling and to drive the Russians out of the emplacement. We went to sleep in the dugout, since we were not ordered to stand guard. We were supposed to have spent the whole night freezing in foxholes near the emplacement.

Later we learned that the battalion special forces had tried to drive the Russians from the emplacement with smoke bombs, but that the water on the floor had doused them. Besides, the bombs could not be thrown far into the emplacement. The passageway leading to its entrance was winding, so constructed that no one could throw hand grenades or satchel charges or smoke bombs of this sort through the entrance.

That night it was decided that a Russian-speaking man should be found, who could shout to the neighbors in the emplacement that they should surrender or have the whole emplacement blown into the air. But not in the whole Laurila regiment nor in all the regiments fighting on the Taipale River sector could a man be found who spoke Russian. Somewhere on the Suvanto shore was Special Battalion 6, a Karelian battalion made up of men from Metsäpirtti. They were asked if any of the Karelians knew Russian, but there was no one who did, not even in that battalion. They sent word that there had been one man who knew Russian, but that he had already been killed in December.

We were left in peace that morning. Many were in an ill humor because the fifth company men had fired on us, and everyone's nerves were getting tight. The platoon leaders were off consulting with the company commander. On his return, our platoon leader told us that they were already convinced that last night's shooting had resulted from the fifth company's confusion and that our reputation was clean.

A request had been sent from the battalion to have Army Corps draw up a paper in Russian from which we could read to the Vanyas in the emplacement exhortations to surrender since no Finn able to shout them in Russian could be found.

In the afternoon we stood in our foxholes looking toward the Kaarna River and the Schoolhouse Woods, waiting for the Russians to try something again. We could hear fighting going on in Terenttilä and Kirvesmäki. A couple of hundred Russians rose from the Kaarna River channel and began walking calmly toward the Pärssinen woods. We could not understand by what route they had gotten into the Kaarna River channel. They walked as calmly as if they were going about the business of peace, dragging machine guns behind them.

We began firing on them with all our weapons and notified the artillery and mortars of their position. The Russians got into a real hurry when hundreds of weapons opened fire on them. They began running in every direction around the field. Many of them died there. But some of them got into the Pärssinen woods, and when the field was empty of living Russians we began to puzzle over where they could have come from. We came to the conclusion that they must have got lost and thought they were in some totally different place when we opened fire on them.

It was quiet for a time. We were able to eat the food that was brought to us. Then the men on watch came shouting that the Russians were again at our tank barriers at the mouth of the Kaarna River. We had to leave our food and run to our positions. Our mortars were already trying to fire toward the mouth of the Kaarna River. The Russians did not lie still under that fire, but began attacking toward the Meadow emplacement. There were two hundred of them, and they were bent on taking possession of the emplacement, but they didn't get far into the field before our artillery began an interdicting fire in front of them and our mortars to fire right into their midst. Our neighbors had no tanks with them at all. They were forced to turn and head for home. We fired all we could at them from the flanks and the boys near the emplacement fired at them too.

When they turned and ran toward the Pärssinen woods, their own mortars were firing in front of and into them, so that their way home was blocked. Now they turned toward us again in total panic and tried to come into our positions, but they had no entry there either. We kept firing at them with rifles and machine guns and they started running back and forth in the field between the Kaarna River and the Pärssinen woods, where there was no shelter for them. They were chopped up by their own mortars and all our fire and a whole lot of them died there. A few got back to their own side.

During the confusion of that fighting, four Russians had again run out of the Meadow emplacement. Our boys shot two of them. The Russian artillery fired on the terrain there all afternoon and inflicted heavy losses on our men who were stationed around the emplacement. Their hastily dug positions could not withstand such fire. We lost twenty men dead and wounded. The Meadow emplacement turned out to be very costly to us as well as to our neighbor.

During the artillery concentration the battalion commander's adjunct had tried to throw a paper printed in Russian to those inside the emplacement urging them to surrender. He had also shouted in Russian what it said on the paper, but no one had answered. Not a single Vanya had come out. No one really knew if there were any Russians left in the emplacement, but it was decided to keep watch on it.

Late in the evening we attempted to attack the emplacement,

but the attack got nowhere because the Russian artillery kept up a constant fire on it. We had to wait until the following day to see if the fire would let up enough so that we could drive out the Russians. If there were any there — no one could say for sure.

However, the artillery fire did not let up on the following day and we could not attack the emplacement. In the afternoon the Russians opened fire with such a large gun that the emplacement collapsed completely, leaving only a crushed heap of concrete and twisted iron.

We were near the emplacement then, waiting for the fire to let up enough for us to attack and take the Russians left in it prisoner, but the collapse of the emplacement made that impossible. So we never got to know if there still were any of our neighbor's boys in it. Our company commander sent a message to battalion saying that the Meadow emplacement had collapsed so completely that only an archeologist would go into it now.

We returned to our own positions, blessing our luck that our turn to try a thrust into the emplacement had not come; it would have been awkward to get into, especially if the neighbor's men had been there with a rifle barrel sticking out toward us.

That night we were relieved from the Joensuu sector. It was again the Central Finland men's turn to attend to our country's business there. It was the Lieksa battalion that took our positions.

XXV

We were now taken to rest at the Koveroja base, which had been a rest area since the beginning of the war. The lodging there was poor. We arrived at night on the seventeenth of January when it was bitter cold, 30 below, and we were all tired and hungry and louse-ridden, in dirty and ragged clothes. We had been forced to go ten days without a bath, except for attempts to scrub our hands and face with snow. A person doesn't get very clean with that kind of bath.

There were too few dugouts for us at Koveroja. On the first night we were packed into unheated dugouts and tents. They could not be heated during the day because the Russian air arm was over us all the time. It would have been easy for them to spot the smoke from stoves in the daytime and start bombing our lodgings. So at first we had to put up with the stinging chill in unheated, packed quarters.

We began at once to build new dugouts and a delousing sauna for the battalion in order to live a little more comfortably and get rid of our lice and bedbugs. They breed so quickly in a war when one can't bathe or wash one's dirty clothes. We often wondered where these extra domestic animals came from. We really had none in civilian life, but after only a week at war everyone was covered with them. They were such a plague that sometimes during an attack a man found himself hoping the Russians would let up long enough for him to scratch himself. These bedbugs and lice were like bacteria or seeds waiting for war to break out. Only then did they begin growing and multiplying. When the second war broke out I noticed the same thing.

So we built a delousing sauna where we singed the surplus lodgers from our clothing. We bathed at night too and tried to scrub ourselves free of the dirt we had accumulated on the Joensuu sector. The ten days there at Koveroja passed quickly, the first few in a kind of sleepy daze. We started building dugouts there, but finished only a few before we again had to leave for the Taipale River. None of us got to live in them. They were left for the men from Central Finland who were coming from the Taipale River for their rest period.

Our company was also called upon to organize the air watch at Koveroja. We had to crouch there during the day counting the Russian planes. There was a lot of counting to do. There might be fifty to sixty bombers in one flight ferrying their loads to drop on the necks of the Finns at Terenttilä and Kirvesmäki and the whole Taipale sector. Large formations of Russian planes flew over every day on the way to bombing targets in Vyborg and the interior of Finland. The planes were a real headache to us. We yearned for our own planes in the sector to give us something to battle the Russian planes with. An army rifle was pretty useless against them, although we used ours to bang away at the planes. We often heard stories about planes being downed with a rifle somewhere on the front. I never saw it happen, but I heard the stories often. Somewhere farther west in the Summa area a rifleman was said to have downed a bomber. That's what they said.

In February the first battalion got so tired of the overwhelming strength of Russian planes that they decided to buy their own plane and pay their own flyer to defend the Taipale sector. They decided that their plane would fly over the Taipale River every day to fight against the Russian planes there and try to protect the infantry. A collection taken up in the first battalion amounted to forty thousand in current markkas. I don't know what a pursuit plane cost then. Even Matti Laurila waxed enthusiastic about the collection. He notified the other battalions that it would be worth their while to start collecting money for their own planes. Our battalion took up the idea, and we all put in money. We were still collecting toward the end of February when we were resting again in back of the lines, ready to be thrown back into the battles at the Taipale River. But then we had to leave for Vuosalmi. We never did get to buy the plane, nor did I ever hear what happened to the treasury; we never got the money back, and many a boy who contributed was no longer there to receive it.

On the twenty-third of January we were informed that a Russian prisoner had been taken who said that a large-scale attack was beginning at Suvanto. Our regiment was immediately put on the alert to carry out a counterattack if the Russians broke through the Suvanto line. We broke ski trails from Koveroja to the places where our company would launch a counterattack in case of a breakthrough. We could see that the Kirvesmäki sector was very hard to defend. The men of Central Finland had been fighting there for the entire Winter War. They'd had a tough time of it. Their positions were thoroughly battered by artillery, as was the entire terrain of the Kirvesmäki sector. They told me they had lost a lot of boys. Their dugouts were all shot to pieces and the woods there had been laid flat by the artillery. They also knew that the Russians were planning a big attack and would try to break through with large numbers, but they were firm in their belief that the Russians would not get through. Later I heard that Yrjö Jylhä, a poet and writer from that Kirvesmäki landscape, had been a company commander there. He wrote a collection of poems about the war there and called it "Fires of Purgatory."

We skied back over the trails we'd made and sat around on the alert waiting for the command for the counterattack. It was a miserable and nerve-racking sort of waiting. We didn't know if the order would come, and if it did come, who would manage to ski back alive and whole.

It wasn't until morning that we heard the Russians had begun the battle at Suvanto. We went outside the dugout to listen to how long it would go on, waiting every moment for them to come and tell us to get ready to join in. We waited the whole morning and afternoon, but the command to counterattack did not come. We assumed that the men from Central Finland still had not let the Russians through at Taipale. Many of us blessed them silently in our minds.

In the evening we were ordered to go and dig open the trenches that had been covered over. Two platoons from our company had to go, and ours was one of them. We skied to Kirvesmäki and set to work. The Central Finlanders dug along with us, for the trenches were vital to their staying alive. They told us about the Russian attacks that day and how many Russians had died and how many of their own boys had been lost.

We carried away the bodies and body parts out of the trenches and spent the whole night digging out those that had been filled in. As we dug we kept finding more bodies and body parts and moving them out of the way. After digging, we braced and strengthened the trenches with sandbags. Toward morning the men of Central Finland went to their dugouts to sleep. They expected that a hard day's work lay ahead of them. They slept a few hours, but not their officers, who stayed awake the entire time. The men on guard stayed awake in their holes too, scanning the ground out front. Here the Russians had already begun digging toward the Finnish positions in December; they dug zigzag trenches into which we could not fire from our positions. As we were opening up our trenches, we could hear the Russians working close to us in the darkness of the night.

Our battalion, in fact the whole regiment, spent the remainder of the rest period waiting to counterattack and repairing these trenches at Terenttilä and Kirvesniemi. During the day we tried to sleep in cold and crowded dugouts and tents. Only those troops designated as backup at Koveroja were able to build dugouts. We had an order that if the Russians attacked at night when we were in the front lines digging out the trenches, the group that was at the point of attack was to begin fighting the Russians along with the Central Finland men. The rest were to gather their things at once and ski back to Koveroja, since the breakthrough might come at any point and there had to be some of us ready at once to be thrown in front of the boys from the steppes.

We did have to snatch up our guns a few times while we were digging, but mostly the Russians did not try to attack at night during January. They assembled large detachments to attack in the morning, but at night only patrols came out past the lines. It was their task to find out what the Finnish boys were up to in their positions, if they were tired of the war and ready to make peace. The patrols did fire on us and that kept us alert, but they did not try to come into our positions. I heard that they captured some men who were on guard, but I never happened to be there where it happened.

Little was done toward building our own dugouts. The back-up detachments didn't get much done in a night, and we couldn't work at all during the day because of the enemy planes.

At night when we came back to Koveroja from our positions, we tried to cover all our tracks and the trails which had developed in the Koveroja dugout area overnight. The dugout builders covered their work up with snow for the day so that the Russians would not see them either from their planes. When the switch was made, the men from Central Finland got into new, louse-free dugouts, for there had been time to finish some of them. We too had been able to wash ourselves clean during the time we rested at Koveroja. We killed off the lice and other vermin in the delousing sauna, but it didn't take many days back in the front lines before every man was again scratching himself with both hands.

XXVI

On the twenty-sixth of January we again got the order to march to the front lines and take the place of the Central Finland regiment, which had held the Russians at bay for ten days.

Our battalion was again held in combat reserve. We were lodged in tents back of the front line at Terenttilä. Our tasks were to dig open the trenches that the Russian artillery and air arm had blocked up, and also to attack wherever the Russians had succeeded in breaking through in our regimental sector of the front. That was the intention. Laurila's battalions, however, had shrunk to very little. Boys were being lost constantly and replacements no longer came at the same rate as they were lost to Russian fire. And now our platoons were constantly being detached for the use of the first and third battalions. They were, in effect, taking part in the fighting.

Our first days were quiet, for the Russians were still not attacking our positions with their infantry. But their artillery fire was already terrible. It chewed up the earth to black mud and mowed down the last of the trees beyond the Terenttilä field. Now we received an order from Laurila to station riflemen in trees, crack shots, who were to shoot Russians as they were digging trenches toward our lines or moving about carelessly in their positions. It must have been Matti Laurila and Antti Isotalo, his infantry buddy from Härmä, who came up with this notion. Isotalo was Laurila's adjutant at regimental headquarters. He'd been through many wars and family feuds. But we had to tell those infantry warriors that there was not a single tree left standing on the fringes of the field into which a sharpshooter could climb to spy out the Russians. So the order was withdrawn. Conditions had been a little different on the eastern front during World War I, when Laurila and Isotalo most likely had seen sharpshooters posted in trees.

Information came from the front lines about truckloads of Russian troops being driven to Koukkuniemi and about other lively traffic beyond the Taipale River. We figured the quiet spell would not last long, that the Russians would soon come charging forward, and that the heavy artillery fire was preparation for something ugly. The fire was so severe that we had to be forever shoveling out the front-line trenches to keep them from being filled in. We took many casualties from shrapnel at this work, but I don't recall anyone's being killed during those days.

It was on the evening of the twenty-ninth that the Russians started moving under cover of heavy fire from their artillery. They crossed the field and took possession of the Mustaoja base, killing all the men there. The Russian artillery kept up such a heavy fire on all of Terenttilä and the Mustaoja base that the boys of the first battalion had no chance to counterattack. They were not even certain who had possession of Mustaoja.

The regimental commander was then Major Lilius, since Matti Laurila had been appointed temporary commander of the whole Taipale sector. The Ostrobothnian officers did not work at all well with this Lilius. He dithered every which way about the Mustaoja base. He ordered a reserve battalion alert and we sat in our tents all night in battle gear. Then came an order from Major Lilius that we were to go to the front line to dig trenches, since the Mustaoja strong point was safely in our hands. When we were just about to leave the tents, a new order arrived, this time from the battalion commander. Now we were to come to Mustaoja ready for a counterattack. Our men were not in the base at all. The Russians were there.

Our company was ordered to carry out a counterattack. We moved out early in the night, as soon as the company commander had returned from reconnoitering Mustaoja for points of attack. We all had skis, and we skied for some distance on ready-made trails, then left our skis and started toward the Mustaoja base on foot. The Russians fired a mortar concentration right into our midst: it's a wonder that only one of our boys was wounded. When we came to the first Mustaoja strong point it was already in our hands. The Russians had been driven from it to their own lines. The first battalion commander then arranged with our company commander to leave one of our platoons at the Mustaoja base to help the first battalion, which had suffered heavy losses in retaking the strong point. The rest of our company was allowed to go back to where the battalion was quartered. It had been a useless trip for us, but we didn't complain.

The constant Russian artillery fire, the bombing from the air, and the pressure from the infantry were making things difficult in the front lines. Battalion ranks were thinning out and no replacements were coming in. A command came down from the regiment for us to send a whole company to the first battalion. They had very few men left and had received no replacements except for those from the regiment's reserve battalion, which should have been used for counter-attacks to throw back the enemy at breakthrough spots. Our company was not involved in that task. That fell to the battalion's fifth company, the boys from Ylihärmä.

Things got tough for the Ylihärmä boys, who were involved in defending the Mustaoja strong points. We had to take their place at the third Mustaoja strong point in the early morning hours of January thirty-first. The heavy Russian artillery fire and the constant pressure of the infantry had kept them from sleeping or getting any food for two days and nights. One of our platoons was sent to let the boys from Ylihärmä go and get some rest.

The next day the Russians tried to attack the strong point where our company's boys were, but the attack seemed feeble. The only result was some dead Russians. Forty of them died there and we were able to collect their papers and war materiel. They had come running at us and had fallen close to our positions. That's what the boys from our company told us when we came to dig the trenches open in the evening. None of our boys was lost that day, even though the Russian artillery kept firing all day long. We dug the trenches open all night. It was very quiet, but very cold.

The rest of our stint on line was spent in opening blocked trenches and digging new ones. We took a turn at strong point number three. The early days of February were quiet on the Taipale sector. Although the Russians fired their artillery and mortars constantly and airplanes came to bomb the sector, they did not really try to come into our positions with the infantry. "The usual artillery fire at The Taipale River" was the headquarters' situation report during the entire time.

A story went around at this time that five Russian parachutists had been captured in back of the lines, and that one of them was a woman. Or rather, they had been shot there because they had not known the password and had fired on our men. They were all wearing Finnish Civil Guard uniforms and had Finnish identification papers in their pockets. Their weapons were of Russian make. At first our men had a scare, thinking they had killed some of our own when they approached the bodies and saw the Finnish dress and looked at their papers; only later when they noticed the Russian weapons had they calmed down, especially when they saw that these dead neighbor parachutists had their chests covered with Guard's marksmen's medals and Finnish honorary ribbons. None of our own men had any of these. Few had decent clothes, much less tokens of honor, to wear.

Once when coming toward the Mustaoja strong point in the evening darkness we ran into a single man who could not give the password even though we asked him for it. We didn't shoot the man right away for having forgotten the password. He fled and managed to get away even though we fired after him. He must certainly have been one of them.

On the morning of February sixth we were again relieved of front-line duty and brought back to the Concentration Camp rest area. It got that name because the enemy artillery had been firing heavy concentrations on it during the entire war. There was not a single tree standing intact there, and the earth was chopped up by shells, like a badly plowed field. The dugouts there were firmly built and sound.

XXVII

After coming at night to the Concentration Camp and getting a little rest, we began our stint in rear reserve by going to the dugout village on the north side of the Terenttilä field to build new dugouts for the combat reserve there. We spent the whole day doing it. It was quite cold, and the Russian artillery fired on our work site all day long. We didn't get much done, digging in the hard ground under artillery fire. We were at the dugout site the next day as well.

On the eighth of February we again set out for the dugout site early in the morning, but before we reached it, an order came to return to the Concentration Camp and be on alert there. The Russians had again launched an attack in Terenttilä, a very powerful attack. They forced their way into the Central Finlanders' positions and completely took over two Mustaoja strong points, pushing even beyond them into the Terenttilä swamp. The men of Lagerlöf's battalion tried to push the Russians out of the strong points and drive them back from the Terenttilä swamp, which was far behind our lines, but they did not have enough men to do it.

The order arrived from battalion toward evening and we skied as far as Virstahovi where we stopped. There we waited a long time, freezing and listening to the sounds of fighting from the direction of Terenttilä. It wasn't fun to hear, there were so many weapons sounding off, artillery and infantry weapons. I started to feel as if I no longer cared about anything. I just wanted to keep warm but I was freezing all the time. I didn't want to think that they would soon order us to move. The boys had little to say there.

Järvinen, the battalion commander, came and explained the situation to our officers. We set out, circling the branches of Terenttilä swamp until we came to where the Central Finlanders had been driven when the Russians seized their strong points and a part of the Mustaoja gully. We were ordered to attack that gully and drive the Russians out of it.

We spent that whole day and until noon of the following day trying to drive out the Russians, but we could not do it. Every last man of our battalion who could stand up was thrown into the counterattack — the cooks, messengers, the supply men, every one who could hold a rifle. The breakthrough at Mustaoja was that bad. The Russians could have come through the entire Taipale sector from there.

In the attack on the Mustaoja gully, we drove the Russians before us toward the Taipale River, but we didn't get far because the other units were of no help to us. They lagged far behind. The Lieksa battalion did not even start out. There were really only about eighty men left in it. And we had no artillery strikes worth mentioning. The fifth company was supposed to take Mustaoja strong point number one from the Russians but they failed. We ran out of cartridges in the counterattack. We had to leave the gully and come back to the Terenttilä swamp and lie there, miserable, in a swamp ditch all night. Toward morning the Russians began firing along the ditch with a machine gun. It was a miserable place to try to hang on to ones' life. We tried to dig hollows in the sides of the ditch deep enough so we'd have some chance of survival when the Russians cut loose along it with their machine guns.

The cold was awful. Our battalion commander froze his feet there, and many others froze their feet and hands. We lost a hundred men from our battalion on that one night and morning, dead and wounded and frostbite victims. The battalion commander was wearing his gentleman's boots, tight-topped jazz boots, which were poor protection against the cold in a temperature of forty below. His feet were so badly frozen that they had to haul him away on a sled. I heard that a boy from Ylistaro, whose own feet were even more badly frozen than Captain Järvinen's, pulled the sled. First Valtonen took over as our battalion commander, and then Pitkänen, and later Sihvo, who died at Vuosalmi.

We were replaced at noon in the Terenttilä swamp drainage ditch, a difficult operation because the Russians controlled the entire ditch. They were within twenty meters of our foremost men, but our entire company got out alive and was able to get back to the Concentration Camp area.

The following day we spent making barbed-wire mounts, which were set out before our rear defensive line at Terenttilä. We made them for many days, all the while we were in rear reserve. We made many hundreds of them. For some reason I remember that. The Russians attacked fiercely during those days, and our battalion was often on alert, waiting for a command to go to the front lines, but we were not needed again on the Taipale River line. We sat in fear in the dugouts during artillery concentrations. The dugouts at the Concentration Camp were well built. The boys even built a sauna in these quarters and we were able to bathe at night. We did not lose any men there.

On the fifteenth of February we got a complete rest. We set out marching that evening by way of Saapru to the village of Yläjärvi, where we were quartered at night. By then we had been on line at the Taipale River front or in reserve there from early December on, about three months. It was a solemn and quiet march from Taipale to Yläjärvi, for our battalion ranks had been badly thinned out at Taipale and there weren't many left of the boys who had marched along Artillery Road to the Taipale River front near mid-December. I had lost my own brother and many acquaintances and close friends. One thing I wondered at was that time had passed so quickly. I really had to look closely at the calendar in Yläjärvi to believe that two months of my life had rolled by. At the Taipale River you had no time to note time's passing since there was always something that had to be done quickly. And at bottom there was the constant fear of dying.

At Yläjärvi we were lodged in houses. We were able to stay there for two weeks. They started granting us furloughs, and some of the boys got home leaves before the Russians' last big assault on *The Isthmus* began. Then everyone on leave had to come back, their leaves cut short or completely canceled. I applied for a leave too, but it was not granted since there was no pressing need at home.

So I wound up staying at Yläjärvi for two weeks with nothing to do. We listened to the radio news about the progress of the war and we heard the pounding of artillery all the way from the Taipale River although it was a long way off.

Now things took another turn in the war on the Taipale River.

Our place was taken by a fresh but inexperienced regiment that could not take the battle there. The Russians shattered the whole regiment on its first day on line. They began to call it the porcelain regiment because the troops were dressed all in white, in new snow uniforms. Even their weapons had been painted white. Maybe they were called the porcelain regiment for some other reason. We had to give them all the helmets from our regiment because there had been no helmets to distribute to them when they set out. They painted the helmets white too, to better match the porcelain boys' uniforms. Turning over the helmets led us to believe that we would get to rest for a long time, since they wouldn't send us to the front lines without them. We were wrong about that.

At the end of February, the war was becoming impossible. The enemy broke through our lines on the western Isthmus, and at the Summa, Leipäsuo, and Lähde sectors. It was said that on the Lähde sector an entire Swedish-speaking coastal regiment had taken flight, and that the Russians had been able to come through the lines there. I don't know. Later, during the second war, this report of the coastal Swedes taking flight during the Winter War was officially denied.

The Russians were threatening to cut the entire Isthmus and leave the regiments fighting at Taipale badly surrounded. Even we had to leave the village of Yläjärvi in the middle of our rest period and fight the Russians until the end. We would have needed helmets then, but the porcelain boys had all of them.

In our opinion, they would not have needed the white uniforms because the artillery fire and aerial bombing on the Taipale River sector had chopped the ground to black mud. A man in white made a good target there, like a grouse in its white winter dress against the thawed ground of spring. Our boys asked if they were also going to collect all the white horses in the country for the porcelain battalion. But they didn't start the collection.

We were, however, able to stay at Yläjärvi until the twenty-eighth of February, when we had to leave again.

XXVIII

They told us only that the regiment's responsibility would shift to the front line at Vuosalmi, where we would finally be on the Mannerheim Line we had heard so much about. We would take up positions there to hold the line against the Russians.

We marched off in the evening, leaving Yläjärvi and joining the regimental column. It was bright moonlight. We were able to fit most of our equipment onto sleighs and trucks, so we had to carry only our own rifles and personal gear. We marched from the village into the woods, the first battalion in the lead. Although it was forty kilometers from Yläjärvi to Taipale, we could already hear the roar of the Russian artillery. It was a continuous rushing sound, as if a huge chimney fire were burning somewhere. You could not make out individual detonations. The sounds of small arms fire did not carry this far. As we marched away from those sounds our thoughts tended to go back to the Terenttilä field, to the Pärssinen, Hiekkala, and Joensuu sectors. How might the boys be doing there? Beyond Yläjärvi the woods were intact and snow-covered. They swallowed up sounds, and the marching of a large group of men gradually drowned out the roar of the artillery.

We came to the shore of a lake. What lake it was, we didn't know. I thought it might not be healthy for us to march across the lake in such bright moonlight since Russian planes flew at night too in such weather. But the men of the first battalion were already far out on it and they could be seen as plainly as in daylight from the shore where we stood resting under the trees. The order came that we were not to start crossing the lake before the first battalion had reached the other side, and we waited until then. Then we started across.

When we were right at the center of the lake, with kilometers to go in either direction, the men in front of us began to dive on their bellies into the snow on either side of the furrow tramped by the column. We had to do the same, although we didn't know why. I lay in the snow and then I heard the sound of airplanes coming closer. Lying there I kept waiting the whole time for the bombs to start exploding and the machine guns to start singing, not daring to look up. We had been given new snow uniforms at Yläjärvi, but we had no helmets, only fur caps and summer hats. I had a helpless feeling, I knew I could do nothing against the enemy. Suddenly it grew darker, a thick curtain of clouds traveled across the sun as the planes flew over us. The boys counted seventy-two of them, bombers and pursuit planes. They flew very low over us, but they did not drop their bomb load on our battalion there on the lake. They had not noticed us. The cloud which had covered the moon began to sprinkle snow, which soon became so heavy that we could not see ahead. Later, as the snow fell, we heard the Russian planes come back and fly toward Russia. By then we were far from the lake in the shelter of the woods.

We came to a road. There was a line of buses there and we were told to board them. We tried to crowd in, men and equipment. Our platoon leader said that the Finnish army took good care of its boys since it had arranged a real bus ride for us at the end of a march. As I recall, it was Erkkilä who spoke. He already knew that a soldier was never offered a ride except when there was a big hurry to get him to plug up a bad hole somewhere. Soldiers always had to pay dearly for a ride.

When they got us loaded, the buses started off at once without lights. We sat there in the dark buses waiting for what the future would bring. It was very cold. Clothing wet with sweat from marching became clammy. I tried to smoke in secret, down close to the floor, and other smokers crouched down too with cigarettes in their mouths. It was slow going through the night. Sleep was out of the question. When you dropped off into some kind of doze, you soon woke up shivering and had to try to move around in that packed bus and rub yourself to get warm. But no one got warm on the whole trip. We tried to eat cold bread and we froze. I was getting disgusted with this traveling and fighting. I felt a rage toward just about everyone and everything.

Around six in the morning we reached our destination. The buses stopped and we were ordered out. We stepped onto the road and tried to loosen up our stiffened joints by hopping up and down on the road and the roadside. We were on the riverbank in Vuosalmi. Across the river was the Äyräpää church village. We could see men running across the ice from there, many of them without guns, bareheaded and ill clad. They were in a state of panic. As they came they shouted that Salmenkaita had been crushed and that nothing could be done to stop the Russians.

"We've always been able to do something," we yelled at them, but they didn't listen. They ran by the hundreds across the river and disappeared into the woods behind the village of Vuosalmi. Their officers tried to get them to stop, but they did not trust their officers' commands. They kept going once they had taken a notion to run.

We had been told that the Russians had come through at Salmenkaita and were now driving the Finns ahead of them, and that if they came through at Vuosalmi, the whole Isthmus would be cut. That meant the whole gang fighting at the Taipale River and holding their own would be caught at the bottom of a sack. We were determined that the Russians would not come through at Vuosalmi, at least if the Mannerheim Line was ready there, a heavily fortified defensive position where we could surely hold our own for a long time.

We marched over the Vuoksi River to the Äyräpää side, with panicky defenders of Salmenkaita streaming toward us all the time. We climbed the bank on the Äyräpää side and were led to a defensive position near the Äyräpää railway station. There was no Mannerheim Line to be seen.

We began burrowing into pits in the snow and gathering logs and branches in front of them as some kind of shelter. It was impossible to dig into the ground because we had no tools. Gangs of men came from the direction of Salmenkaita the whole time, sometimes individual men, and then some vehicles as well, and then the delaying troops. They all felt that we were now helpless against the Russians. The delaying forces were dead tired. I saw this happen — a group of some thirty men came and stopped near the railroad station. They were probably what was left of a company or a battalion. When they stopped marching, the men toppled into the snow and fell asleep there. You simply could not wake them up no matter what you did. They were all asleep. From somewhere their superiors rounded up horses and sleds, loaded the men onto them, covered them with whatever tatters and rags they could find, and carted them off to the other side of the Vuoksi. They were a pretty tired bunch.

Those who were a little more awake told us that the Russian artillery fire at Salmenkaita had been something awful, The cement of the defensive positions there had not had time to dry, and the artillery fire had shattered all the bunkers. The metallic firing cupolas atop the bunkers had flown off in the artillery concentrations like barn swallows taking flight. Then the tanks had come, Russian heavy tanks, with the infantry behind them. Our men had had to flee.

Anyway we thought we would try to slow down the Russian boys here at Äyräpää although we knew enough about war to sense that the place we had been brought to was not easy to defend. We were in unfortified positions with only pits in the snow to protect us, with the ridges of Äyräpää behind us and then the Vuoksi, which was hundreds of meters wide at this point, and beyond the river the fields of Vuosalmi.

Our company commander went around surveying our positions. He said that Sihvo, who had become the battalion commander, had asked Laurila to have us dig in at the edge of the woods on the other side of the river. There it would be easy to shoot the Russians with machine guns if they tried to cross on the ice of the Vuoksi. Laurila had refused. We didn't know why, but we figured he had his reasons.

XXIX

We spent the first day in Äyräpää waiting for the Russians, directing the delaying forces across the Vuoksi, and working on our positions. Many of the troops coming from Salmenkaita told us they were the very last, that the pointed caps were right on their heels, but our own troops kept coming from Salmenkaita all day long. Only toward the end of the afternoon did things quiet down and troops stop coming. Russian planes did fly over Äyräpää and fighter planes fired their machine guns on the opposite bank. They thought we would start resisting them there, that we were digging in on that bank, but we were here on the Äyräpää side and the only ones on the Vuosalmi side were the boys who were fleeing from Salmenkaita. On the Vuosalmi side we had only the third battalion, which was in regimental reserve. The rest of us were around the Äyräpää church and the railway station, and on the islands in the river, Vasikkasaari, Mustasaari, and Dynamosaari.

At night the engineers set fire to the entire village of Äyräpää, which burned brightly, lighting up all the surroundings. They also blew up the church tower, which was too good a target for Russian planes to aim at and a clear directional beacon when they were coming to Äyräpää.

In the evening word also came that replacements had arrived

on the Vuosalmi side, who had to be fetched and shown our positions and distributed to the battalions and companies. I was ordered to be one of the group that went to get the replacements. We went first to the battalion command post, which was in a sauna on the river, in the shelter of the bank. Potila, the battalion commander's adjunct, explained to us where we would find the replacements and how they were to be distributed. There were a few of us from each company getting them and we crossed on the ice to the other side of the Vuoksi. In the bright light from the burning church village of Äyräpää it was easy for us to follow the tracks of sled runners to the other bank.

We went into the first house on that side, lighted a fire in the stove, and made coffee. The house was abandoned, its goods scattered over the floor. Lambs were bleating in the barn. The boys killed one of them, but it was left uneaten. There wasn't time to prepare food. A runner arrived from the third battalion who claimed that the smoke from the fire we had lighted could be seen all the way to Leningrad on a night like this, and that Russian planes would soon put a stop to our coffee-making if we didn't put out the fire. We averred that the Russians already knew that the Finns were occupying positions in Äyräpää since the whole village was burning. We finished making the coffee, then drank it and ate some bread. It was all we got to eat that day, since the field kitchens were still on their way to the Vuosalmi battlefield.

The boys were beginning to roast the lamb, but then they came to get us. We had to cut half-cooked pieces from the leg of lamb to take with us. We were led along the road the buses had taken when bringing us to Vuosalmi that morning. The replacements were in the woods behind the school. There were a couple of hundred of them, some yanked out of their schoolroom desks, and some from older conscription groups. One of the boys said he had managed to get eight days of training in the art of war at a training center before bring forced to head for Vuosalmi. We took them over the river to their positions. One of the boys asked our platoon leader if he could try firing his rifle. When we wondered why he wanted to start spraying bullets around in the middle of the night, he told us that he had never in his life fired an army rifle. He wanted to try it and see if it kicked as hard as they had said it would. He was not given permission to fire, but was told to wait, that he would soon see something to shoot at. He did not live long on that ridge at Äyräpää.

An order came to watch the Salmenkaita road to see when the enemy were coming. There had been no sign of them yet. Our platoon leader said that for once we should take some older men. They'd always been too willing to send younger men on these reconnaissance trips. The casualty rate on them tended to be high, and we'd lost many boys.

Some ten of us went, with the platoon leader in charge, and we walked down that road as freely as if we were going to a dance. We kept going until someone ahead asked us just who we were and did we know the Finnish password. Some of our own engineers were still out there booby-trapping the terrain. We had known nothing about them. We might have shot them all if we had noticed them earlier. They told us that there was still another group of engineers up ahead mining the road, and not to shoot them.

But we did not see any more of our own troops. A Russian mounted patrol came toward us, most likely on the same errand as we were: we looked for a place where we might stop and make a stand against them. We asked for the password, but they had

164

their own. They started firing on us and we returned the fire. Then both sides headed back to their own lines.

Back at our position we sent word to the battalion that the Russians were on their way and that we had seen some of our own engineers who were still out toward the Salmenkaita road. That information caused such a mixup in the third company that when the Russian spearhead arrived, the boys let them walk in complete peace to the banks of the Vuoksi near the church. They mistook the Russians for our engineers. The Russians simply walked through the lines without saying a word. When asked for the password, they did not answer, but the third company boys let them walk through. They thought the Russians were engineers in a bad temper after digging positions and laying mines for many days and nights. It was only when the Russians reached the river-bank that they took a closer look. Then they started shooting, but the Russians sneaked back to their own lines under cover of dark-ness. A whole platoon of them had been there. They too must have been uncertain about the situation, thinking the Finns had run far away. But we had stayed in Äyräpää. We felt that the Russians would get no farther.

The first night in Äyräpää was another night of waiting. Russian detachments did come from the direction of Salmenkaita, but they showed no sign of breaking through our lines at the time. They already knew we were waiting for them and that a battle would be fought on the ridges of Äyräpää. They did make minor attacks throughout the night, but it was only a matter of coming up toward our positions and spraying a few bullets to see how we defended ourselves. Then they always turned back again.

They had no tanks at all with them on the first night and the attacking units were small. We did hear the Russians driving many kinds of motor vehicles farther to the rear, putting artillery into place, and bringing tanks along the road to Äyräpää. Those sounds told us that the neighbor now had strength backing him up. Already in February at the Taipale River we had found in the pockets of dead tank commanders new directives with instructions to change the way of using tanks to support the infantry. The new directive mandated that tanks no longer advance in an open line, as they had throughout January in crossing the Terenttilä field, always with a platoon of infantry behind them. They were all to concentrate on some breakthrough point, the tanks to drive through the Finnish lines and the infantry to follow and broaden the breach in both directions. It was an intelligent plan. In that way they had broken through the Summa and Lähde sectors, and at Salmenkaita. We believed that with this method they intended to break through here as well, but we figured there was a different breed of men facing them here at Äyräpää than at Summa and Salmenkaita. The terrain here was different too.

At the Taipale River we had come to the conclusion that this tank weapon of the Russians was no great problem, but we could do nothing about the artillery. It was always out of sight and beyond the reach of our weapons. Their air arm was overpowering compared to ours. Against the artillery and bombers we could do nothing.

We had to wait all that night there near the Äyräpää station. During that time we could hear the sounds of firing, small skirmishes, and then the third company's battle on the river bank with the Russians they had mistaken for engineers. There was firing behind us and firing ahead of us, and the sounds of vehicles being driven from the direction of the Salmenkaita road. We did not hear any of the engineers' mines exploding. The Russians must have cleared them all.

166

When morning began to dawn, the boys said they would leave their positions long enough to go and make coffee on the other side of the Vuoksi. We'd had no hot food in two days. A person needs something hot after standing nights in a pit in the snow. The platoon leader forbade them to go because he thought the Russians would attack at dawn and that all the men should be in position to repel the attack. But the boys were too tired and cold to listen or to care about the order. Three men from our platoon left, and less than half an hour had gone by when the Russians began a massive artillery bombardment of the village of Vuosalmi on the other side of the river. Apparently they still believed that our real positions were on that side, that we had not left the open spaces of the river and fields behind us to fight on the ridges of Äyräpää. We watched the artillery fire chew up the earth and woods. Roofs and chunks of log walls flew everywhere. The platoon leader said that someone should go and see what had happened to the boys, to see how their coffee-making was coming along. But they were to come back at once to meet the first onslaught of the Russians.

Two of us took off. As we crossed the river, the Russian artillery was still laying it on the village of Vuosalmi. The river ice was full of crevices and holes chopped in it by the artillery. When we reached the other bank, the artillery stopped and we went to the house we'd seen the boys enter to make the coffee. As soon as we reached the yard, we saw that things must have gone badly for them. A piece of the roof and of one wall was missing from the house and a thick line of blood ran down the steps, past an outbuilding, and into the woods. A badly wounded boy had run there, but we never found him. In the entry hall was the upper body of one of our boys; his lower body was on the other side of the main room, five meters away. He was dead. In the room lay a man from Soini who had come into our platoon as a replacement the evening before, an older man, whose belly a shell had ripped open so that his guts were outside his body. One of his legs was torn completely off. He was completely delirious and was crying for water. We tried to stitch him up, to put his guts back into him. We could plainly see that he would not live long, but we tried to help him.

The Russian artillery had begun to pound again and in that barrage we dragged the man from Soini to the aid station and left him there. He didn't live long. After the war I visited his grave among the soldiers' graves in Soini. March first was marked down there as the day he died. That day was March first.

A steady stream of wounded was already beginning to arrive at the aid station. It was not a pleasant place to be, for the wounded were groaning in pain and the Russian artillery was firing on the place. So we left to get back to the Äyräpää side where our company was in position.

XXX

We passed the ferry landing on the way from the aid station, and there we could see and hear that the Russians had begun the task of crushing the Äyräpää defense in good earnest. The artillery was now firing on Äyräpää and planes were flying over it. We ran across the river and into the battalion command post in the shelter of the river bank, where artillery shells could not land.

We had no errand at the command post and no one had time to ask what we were doing there in the middle of a war, so we scampered up the bank and dodged from shell hole to shell hole like gophers in that artillery concentration. We came to where our boys were in position and already repelling the Russians' first effort to cross the Vuoksi near the Äyräpää railway station. Their real blow, however, was aimed lower, in back of the church at an island in the river where the men from Isokyrö and Ylistaro were. Tanks drove that way in a column, with infantrymen in their shelter. Only infantry were trying to come into our positions, and although we had only pits in the snow to protect us, it was not a good place for the Russians to come through. They had to crawl over the snowbanks, and the open places were so narrow that they had to come at us nearly in a line. We shot almost all of them there with our infantry weapons. The rest of them withdrew, and we saw them being driven back into our fire. They could not break through here.

Near the church, however, the Russians did get into our positions and the boys had to leave. We saw them running to the river bank below the ferry landing. The Russians brought a direct-trajectory artillery piece to the ridge, from which it could fire along the river bank. The only shelter our men had was on the very edge of the river. That artillery piece was a big problem for us. In the afternoon the first battalion was ordered to drive the Russians away from the church. They took a lot of casualties but managed to drive the piece back from its position atop the ridge. That relieved the situation a little.

The Russian tanks drove freely around Äyräpää the whole day long, firing non-stop, since we still had no anti-tank weapons with us. Then the boys started to attack the tanks with satchel charges and Molotov cocktails. Soon they had set fire to five of them near the crossroads and in back of the church, and the Russian crews began to be careful about where they drove their tanks. They stayed at a distance and did keep firing their guns, but they no longer came right up on us.

Word came from battalion that the Russians were bringing reinforcements to Äyräpää, that our airplanes had seen continuous lines of marching men and trucks and artillery and armored vehicles coming from Leningrad toward Finland and past Salmenkaita toward Äyräpää. It was not pleasant news for us to hear. I too was beginning to wonder if we could do anything against them at Äyräpää. But I came to the conclusion that one could not know in advance. That it was wisest to wait and see.

The Russians did not try to come at the station area any more that day. We could clearly see their artillery firing at Vasikkasaari.

It was no fun to lie in snow pits on a low island like that under artillery fire. Our boys had a bad time of it there. The Russians did not fire on us often, just enough to keep us awake.

We had bread to eat. They promised us that we would get food during the night because they did not dare drive food across the Vuoksi during the daylight hours, but no hot food came the following night either. Out in front of our positions we heard the sound of digging and of vehicles being driven, and shouts in a foreign language. It was the Russians and they no longer cared about concealment. Rather they wanted to show us that men and war machines were coming to cross the Vuoksi, and that anyone who was in Äyräpää and tried to stop them would be swept aside if he wasn't trampled underfoot.

The boys who had gotten leaves at Yläjärvi came to our positions in the morning. They had barely had a chance to get home and turn around when the order to return arrived; they told us that on the home front people were firm in the belief that the Russians had no business in Finland, and that they had no means or magic tricks to smash our defenses. Although they had heard of the fall of Summa and the recall of everyone to his unit, the people at home believed that the Russians had embarked on a game they could not get out of with honor. No one had believed the boys when they told them what it was like in the Mustaoja gully at the Taipale River and at Terenttilä in January and February; they thought the terrible cold helped us and hurt the Russians. They did not believe that the Russians were accustomed to such bitter weather or could wage a war in such a cold winter, at least not against the Finns, who had been accustomed to the cold since childhood. The papers had even written of it: "King Winter has come to the aid of the Finns."

But when the boys saw our position alongside the railway station there in Äyräpää, when they saw the pits in the snow and heard the din and the babbling in Russian out in front of our positions, they said they figured we would be wiser to head back home. They had eaten and slept so they were still able to mouth off.

They told of meeting one of our pilots at home. He had come down between the lines some time ago here on *The Isthmus*, making a forced landing in a field. On one side were Russian positions and on the other side, Finns. The Finns were from a coastal Swedish-speaking parish and had just been brought to the lines. When the pilot got out of his plane and crawled across the field, both sides fired on him. The Finns from the coast thought the plane was Russian, and so they fired. The Russians fired because they knew the plane was Finnish. But anyway the pilot got into a hay barn in the field. He had to stay in the hay barn all day long. Men shouted something at him from both sides, something he could not understand. He did not know which was the Finnish side. It wasn't until evening that a Finnish-speaking second lieutenant came to the coastal Finland-Swedes' lines and shouted across the field that they would come to get him from the barn at night when it was dark enough.

Lying in the barn, pistol in hand, bleeding heavily at first from his wounds, the pilot decided to fire at anyone who came toward the barn from either side. He would keep firing as long as he was able and then shoot himself. When the second lieutenant shouted to him in Finnish that the Finns would come to get him at night, his first reaction was a great sense of relief. But then, even though the man had shouted his name and rank and had spoken Finnish, the pilot began to wonder if he was telling the truth. There might be Russians who spoke Finnish on either side of the field. So he

172

decided to defend himself with his pistol against anyone who came. During the afternoon, however, he grew weaker from the cold and loss of blood. When it was dark, the coastal Swedish-speakers came to get him. Hearing them babble questions at him in a strange language, he meant to kill them all and then shoot himself, but he was unable to lift a finger. They put him on a sled, covering up the pistol, and pulled him back across the field to their own lines. They had no idea how close they came to dying that night.

We told the boys that here we knew where the enemy was, that we had been facing death, and that soon they would be. The sounds the Russians made seemed at first to come from a few dozen yards away, and then from farther off. They seemed to be everywhere, and it was no fun listening to them. All we could do was wait for what would happen. I was very thirsty and ate so much snow that my mouth burned. Day began to dawn.

XXXI

Iron rained down on us from the morning on. The Russian air arm was over us all the time. It picked up its loads in Leningrad and dumped them on Äyräpää, then flew to pick up a new load and returned to dump it on our heads. The artillery fire was heavy all day, but the Russians did not try to get into our positions until the afternoon. Till then we had to lie there in fear. During all that time the sounds of a non-stop battle came to our ears from the church and from the island. The Russians were trying in earnest to break through at those points and to cross the river by way of the islands, but only in the afternoon did they try to break through near the station.

I don't know if by then they'd had enough of beating their heads against the wall in the churchyard and at Vasikkasaari, since now they tried in large numbers to come through our positions. Neither their artillery nor their tanks any longer had mercy on their own forces. Only when their troops reached our lines did they stop firing, or shift their fire farther back, to the area between the Vuoksi and the station. The first Russians to thrust into our positions died from their own artillery and the direct-trajectory fire of their tanks, but the remainder of them came close up on us. There were many of them and few of us.

We did not consider the pits in the snow a defensive line worth sacrificing our lives for, and we drew back. By now we'd been awake for two days and nights on poor food. Every man was in a kind of daze, not truly knowing much about this world, and not caring. We did fight a kind of hand-to-hand battle with the Russians in those snow pits, but it was only a kind of thrashing around on our part. When we left, the Russians were content with getting our positions and did not start running us to the bank of the Vuoksi. That saved our lives. We dug new pits on the edge of the swamp and from the swamp toward the ski-jump hill and started to defend them. The company commander sent us word that men were on the way from the reserve battalion to help us, that we must not let the Russians get to the riverbank, for that would be the end of us all.

With the men from the reserve battalion came a written order from Laurila that we had to drive the Russians out of our old snow pits near the station. No one said anything to that, there was nothing to say. We were in a kind of daze. The officers began to plan how to carry out the attack — our company commander and the platoon leaders and the officers of the companies released from the reserve battalion. There were no telephone connections in any direction. We were told that the army corps was working to get us messenger dogs to transmit orders and requests, but the dogs had not arrived yet. I had a bit of doubt that dogs were creatures wise enough to trot sheets of paper from here to there, to the right address, like mail carriers. Or to come out alive from an artillery concentration any better than a man, who at least has a brain in his head and can search out some kind of hollow in the ground for protection during the worst explosions. Messengers still had to take care of the dog's function for us: to take messages to the artillery. Our company commander sent a messenger running to Major Sihvo's command post. We were left waiting for our own artillery to remind the Russians that they did not own the pits in the snow they were in, that they had come too far onto Finnish land. But the messenger came back and said that our artillery would not start firing on the Russians lying in our snow pits because they had specific orders to try to stop the tanks that were now gathering opposite the church yard. At the regiment they were afraid that the Russians would get possession of the churchyard. From there they would be able to sweep all our positions with their direct-trajectory guns.

We had to make the attack without any artillery support. The officers placed ballplayers and other good grenade throwers in the van, along with the men who had machine pistols. Then they ordered us to move forward. Our former snow pits were not a good place for the Russians to defend either. Although they had tried to deepen and improve them, we were able to drive them out. The Russians hadn't expected us to return. They thought the new rules of the game called for them to attack and for us to run.

They could not withstand our attack, but rose from the snow pits and ran away along the railroad track. We did get into our old positions again, but both sides lost men. The afternoon was drawing to its end. We were not left in peace for a long time. The Russians again began to drop artillery fire on us. We lost more boys in that fire than in the two attacks made on the snow pits that day, the Russian attack and ours.

I began to think that a fourth night in a row without sleep would fall to our lot. The Russians were very close and they were busy with something out in front of our positions. There was no chance to switch troops even if we'd had any to switch. I wondered if

Laurila could have any men left in reserve.

I lay down and tried to keep from freezing. I couldn't help falling asleep but I woke up again when an artillery shell thumped very close to me. I was no longer sure if I was awake or asleep. I seemed to be dreaming most of the time, a dream which continued without a break through periods of wakefulness. Its story line was unbroken.

Even sleep-walking, no matter how brief, revives a person. It revivified me too that in my sleep I did not have to be on the Äyräpää ridge in Karelia. Mostly I was in familiar places at home, doing the work of peacetime.

The nature of the Russian artillery fire was now such that you could not tell whether they were firing a concentration or paving the way for an attack or merely sending harassing fire our way. It was becoming almost a single sound, a wall.

At about eight or nine the Russians again began coming at us. It was already getting dark and we had been in those snow pits so long that dying no longer seemed to matter. We did the work of killing, which we had been practicing so long, with mechanical precision. There was not a thought in our heads, except perhaps for a slight bewilderment that our neighbor did not seem to believe that he could not get through here. I saw our squad leader standing against a tree firing a Russian machine pistol. Nothing seemed to matter to him. I yelled to him to throw himself down, otherwise he would not last long, but he didn't hear me. Or else he didn't care. Afterwards the boys talked about how amazingly long he stood there rattling off bursts with a machine pistol at the waves of Russians running through the snow. He would stop shooting only long enough to change a clip. He must have been firing for at least a quarter of an hour when a Russian machine gun chopped him to mush. It's hard to estimate time under such conditions. And no one had a chance to look at his watch.

The Russians did get into our snow pits, but only near the center of our line. Both of our flanks lasted out the attack and we had to spend the next night in that situation. I could see that with our neighbor some ten meters away we would not get to spend that night in peace. We couldn't be sure if he intended to expand his position. We had to watch him the entire night, to be on guard for our lives. Every time we awakened from a half-daze or doze, we were afraid that our positions were in enemy hands, that we were prisoners and would soon be dead. That fear warmed us a little. That was the only warmth we had.

The company commander crawled along our line and ordered someone to take word of the situation here to Sihvo at the battalion command post and to ask for more men to hold off the Russians. He said he had already sent many men to carry the message, but no one had come back. So he did not know if Sihvo had received the message. No one could decide whether to go or to stay in the snow pits. The Russians heard our murmur of talk in their own pits and tossed a few hand grenades at us, but they missed our pits in the dark and burst in the snow.

The company commander complained that he could not see who was lying there in the dark. He poked me in the side, and asked who I was. I said my last name.

"Martti or Paavo?" he asked.

"Martti. Paavo was cut in two at Taipale," I said. The company commander said he remembered that, and ordered me to go and tell Sihvo that the Russians were in our positions but that we would drive them out as soon as it grew light and the workday began, and that the battalion might send us a couple of platoons to help us with the job. He told me to try to stay alive and I started off.

The password is Äyräpää's Ärjy," he said as I crawled out of the pit onto the snow. I tried to keep the word in mind as I crawled backward along the snow. I came into the woods, but I was unable to stand up and start walking. So I crawled as far as Kattilasuo. The boys of the headquarters company were there securing our daytime positions.

"Who goes there?" they asked.

"Äyräpää's Ärjy," I said. They lifted me to my feet and pointed out what might be the best way to the river. I walked slowly through the woods until I came close to it. The Russians were sweeping the riverbank with direct-trajectory fire, but I was too exhausted to care about that. I walked upright to its very edge, thinking they would not hit one man when they were aiming at a whole regiment. And they didn't.

I sat on the bank and slid down to the sauna on the river, which was the battalion command post. When I explained my errand, the battalion commander's adjunct promised that they would try to find some men to help us. The commander himself was off somewhere at the company positions. At the command post men kept coming and going and trying to phone all the time. It was warm there and I was about to fall asleep, but I got the feeling that I was in the way so I went out and climbed the slope at an angle upstream the Vuoksi. I found the ruins of a house there with the cellar intact but with debris from the structure lying every which way on top it. There were logs all over the yard, and pieces of the shingled roof strewn everywhere.

I went into the cellar. It was dark and smelled of abandonment. I scratched a match and saw that there were quilts and old bedspreads strewn around the floor. I piled them under and over me so that in the end I was lying completely buried in the old clothes. The Russians were no longer firing at that house.

I thought maybe I could sleep a little. The last sounds I recalled were those of the artillery firing and the explosions of the shells. I remember wondering if a person could fall asleep in that racket. That's all I remember.

XXXII

I woke up to the sound of shouting and sat up in my pile of bedding. I had no idea where I was. I saw the cellar door as a pale opening and heard someone shout something. I yelled "Äyräpää's Ärjy." Someone at the door asked if there were Finns in the cellar; if not, they would throw in a grenade. I stood up in panic and said I was one of theirs. They told me to come out with my hands up and without any weapons. I remembered my rifle and searched for it in the pile of bedding, then walked up out of the cellar.

Outside were boys from headquarters company, men I knew from home. They did not know me at first and kept their weapons trained on me. Having recognized me, they said I might well have died in that cellar. The Russians had come along the ice at night from Mustasaari to our rear. The boys were searching for them now. I told them I had fallen asleep in the cellar in the evening.

I left the headquarters company at the cellar and climbed the bank into the woods. It was about seven o'clock in the morning. I was walking past Kattilasuo in the woods toward our own positions when the Russian artillery again began churning. It seemed as if they were firing at me. I leaped into a shell hole and lay there waiting for the concentration to go past me or off to the side. It did not shift. I began to think that the Russians had decided to kill one man, since I could see no other Finns. I lay in the hole, starting to think I should get word to the Russians to stop bombing this piece of woods since I was the only one here or that's what I thought after I had lain there for some time, afraid that every moment would be my last, the concentration was so heavy. The ground heaved and shook and trees broke and fell around me and shells exploding in treetops rained shrapnel into the snow which sizzled with the heat.

When I had lain there for some time, I got tired of it and began peering out of the hole to see if there were other equally good holes ahead for me to lie in. There were any number of them, and I began dashing from hole to hole until I got out from under the concentration. Then I crawled through the woods along ground chewed up by shells and aerial bombs.

A corporal from our medics came toward me dragging a man with him. I rose and ran to him: he was carrying Erkkilä and at that moment, a Russian artillery concentration opened up on us. Erkkilä was conscious, but delirious. He did not know me at all, just kept shouting, "The Son of God, the Son of God." We tried to roll him into the shelter of a bomb crater. The corporal said one of Erkkilä's arms and one of his legs had been blown off by a shell near the station and he'd lost a lot of blood. We tried to work him into a hole, but before we could, a shell landed close by. When it burst over us, I saw that it had cut off Erkkilä's other leg below the knee. The medic began to bandage it at once. Erkkilä began explaining that he was seeing a being so bright that it almost blinded him, and he kept repeating the words: "The Son of God." He did not live long after that. He never did recognize me.

We agreed to wait in that hole until the Russians shifted their artillery fire somewhere else, since there was no need to hurry with Erkkilä. I promised to help carry him. The medic explained that bodies of our men were being stacked on the river bank and would be moved across the river at night. The wounded they had to try to take back across the river during the day, even though the Russian artillery could fire along it and planes were over it constantly.

We lay in the crater with Erkkilä for a long time. The medic corporal said that the battalion had already lost hundreds of boys during these days: now there were frozen bodies stacked like birch logs along the river. We no longer had Erkkilä to chat with, nor would we ever.

When the artillery fire on the spot let up, we set off to carry Erkkilä, or what was left of him, to the pile of bodies; one arm and leg of his were left at the Äyräpää station and the other leg up to the knee along the way from the station to Kattilansuo. There was no life left in him. When we reached the river bank, the Russians were firing a direct trajectory piece at it and the corporal was badly hit; he flew to one side and rolled into a bomb crater. Erkkilä's body flew in another direction. It seemed to take more iron, his midriff ripped open somehow. I stayed in one piece.

Boys below us on the river bank came up to help. They had a sled with them. I shouted that they need not bother with Erkkilä, that he was a dead man, but that they had to go and see what had happened to the medic corporal. The Russians were keeping up a heavy fire, so it was hard for them to get to the hole where the corporal lay. They had to make their way from hole to hole with the sled. When they reached the corporal, they shouted that he was still alive, but had been badly hit. They found a strange way to bring him back, tossing the sled rope from hole to hole, dashing after it themselves, and then pulling the sled to them. That's how they did it. I watched until they were out of sight behind the bank at the riverside.

I heard later that the corporal told Battalion Commander Sihvo there was no longer any point in hauling dead bodies across the river. There was only one horse left alive. When daylight came, men would be wounded and the horse would be needed to ferry them across. The dead could wait until the following night. Sihvo had given his consent. When the boys brought the corporal to the shore, the horse was there with a sleigh and they started off at a full gallop to take him across the Vuoksi to the Vuosalmi side. He was badly wounded in the abdomen. The Russian artillery kept up a continual fire at the ice on the Vuoksi, and they had to try crossing it in the midst of this concentration: the firing, however, had chopped so many holes in the ice that horse and driver fell into the water. The driver got out and started to run back toward Äyräpää. He was soaking wet and it was freezing cold. The wounded corporal was left lying on the sleigh and managed to roll off onto the ice so that he would not be up on the sleigh directly in the path of bullets. The Russians were then firing on the ice over the Vuoksi with machine guns.

When the driver reached the shore, a man started out from it to put an end to the horse's suffering as it thrashed about in the hole. He was about to shoot the animal, but the wounded corporal was in the line of fire and called out to the man not to kill him in his haste. At that moment four men from Ylistaro ran out from the Äyräpää side, took hold of the horse's harness, shoved the animal completely under the water, then whooped and lifted horse and all up onto the ice. It wasn't the first time they'd pulled a horse from a hole in the ice. One of them leaped up onto the sleigh, took the reins in his hands, and drove across the Vuoksi in the artillery fire. He made it across the river and through the fields to a battalion aid station on the Vuosalmi side. The corporal's life was saved. That's the story they told, after the war was over.

I went running back toward my own company's positions, or rather it was a case of leaping up and hitting the ground time and again, for the Russians were firing on the place the entire time with direct-trajectory weapons from the ridge in back of the church. The boys were in our old position. They told me that the Russians were really ganging up in front of our positions. Sixteen tanks had been counted there, driving back and forth in front of their infantry. We waited for the Russians to start moving.

Artillery fire kept coming all the time. The boys were sure that I had fallen along the way after leaving them in the evening. They had lost a lot of men to artillery fire and in the attack on the Russian positions the day before. The Russians had not given up the positions they had retaken. They had all died there.

All we could do was wait and fear. The Russians began their attack at about ten in the morning, but our artillery fired a concentration of sorts before that, throwing the Russians into confusion, and their infantry attack was badly delayed. They came on without artillery support, and there was little they could do out in the open. Many of them fell; the rest turned back.

In the afternoon at about one o'clock they came on again with tank and artillery support. We fought with them until eight in the evening. Gradually they came to believe that this was a bad place to come into Finland, and at eight in the evening they stopped fighting for that day. We began to look around at the kind of tracks the Russians had managed to leave in our positions and to repair them. We waited for warm food. Six tanks were smoldering and burning in front of our lines and many of our neighbors were lying there. The food did not come. There would also have been a shortage of eaters.

XXXIII

I thought I already knew what a Russian artillery concentration could be like. I'd seen enough of them at Taipale and here at Vuosalmi to think they couldn't be worse. But on the morning of March fourth, I realized that I'd been wrong.

The firing which began at six in the morning was of the usual heavy sort. It hacked at our positions and the terrain behind us as we waited in our pits for what the day would bring. At about nine we saw tanks driving in the direction of the railway tracks with a lot of infantry following. We had captured some prisoners who told us that two fresh divisions had been brought to the front with orders to drive us from the ridge at Äyräpää and out of Vuosalmi. We figured the infantry to be the men from these new divisions; they were coming somehow as if they were not used to war, in their long overcoats, dragging their equipment behind them. We watched as they went past the station toward the Äyräpää church.

At five minutes to ten on March fourth, the Russians showed us what real artillery fire is, when there are plenty of guns and one is serious about using them. It seemed as if the sky fell in on us, all its planets and fixed stars and all the comets that fly around in it. There is no other way to describe it: the frame of the earth changed: it rocked and seemed to rise toward the falling sky and we were caught in between on a stormy sea. And the storm was violent. There was nothing to hold on to, no handhold to grasp. They let the sky rain down on us for a long time, a couple of hours, and their artillery shells were not their regulation kind.

As soon as the concentration began, the battalion command post took a direct hit, although it was supposed to be in a sheltered place on the river bank, in a sauna protected by a slope. In that direct hit we lost the entire battalion headquarters, Battalion Commander Sihvo first of all. His adjunct was to die on the other bank of the river at the platoon aid station. Even as he was dying he kept asking if they were sure word had been sent to Matti Laurila that our battalion commander had been killed and the headquarters destroyed. He was a conscientious man, that Potila.

We did not know anything of this in our positions near the station until early afternoon when the new battalion commander came to see if there was still a single Finnish boy alive in the front lines. The Russians were pouring from there toward the churchyard, trying to take possession of it and the islands below it. It would be better to attack the Finns by hopping across the Vuoksi on the islands rather than on the open ice, where machine guns could sweep them off it.

Now they did not try to attack our positions except in small groups; they kept us pinned down so we were not free to go and help the boys in the churchyard. We lay the whole day in our positions keeping up enough of a fire to make them see that the road this way was closed to them.

All day we watched the battle for the Äyräpää churchyard and the islands. We could see everything clearly and sharply from our positions. The Russians began their attack right after twelve o'clock. After they had softened the place with artillery for a couple of hours, they drove dozens of tanks at it, with infantry by the battalion. But they could not drive out our troops. The boys had made up their minds.

Before noon the Russians had attacked Mustasaari. We had seen some of our men running across the ice to Vasikkasaari and from there to the mainland. The kind of concentration the Russians had arranged for that morning must have made a hash of our positions on the islands, but when they tried to run across from Mustasaari to Vasikkasaari, our boys were still there. All our neighbor's men who tried to switch islands were shot on the ice. We could also see that our boys in the churchyard had a lot of trouble from the planes which flew over Äyräpää as if they were on a training mission with live ammunition. They kept strafing our positions and the ice on the Vuoksi, over which we had to transport our wounded to the aid station across the river. And there were the bombers hauling their bomb loads from Leningrad onto our necks.

But the Russians had decided to take the churchyard from us once and for all, not caring how many men they lost. We lay in our positions and watched from the sidelines while the Russians poured company after company at the churchyard. Each time they were thrown back from the slope a fresh company immediately assembled, attacked, and returned to the tracks with its ranks depleted. That lasted the whole afternoon. The din of killing machines was horrible. No individual sound could be heard, and when the noise had gone on for many hours one felt as if the whole world had changed to a din that reached the threshold of pain.

The Russians again started out from Mustasaari, trying to get to Vasikkasaari. They made it over the sound between the two islands, and now we could see the boys in hand-to-hand combat with them in our positions. The Russians were forced to turn back once more and to run away from Vasikkasaari. Our boys ran after them and managed to drive them off Mustasaari too. The Russians ran from there to the mainland on the Äyräpää side in the grip of panic, throwing their weapons onto the ice and into the bushes along the shore. Our men were already so tired they could not take the whole island, but lay resting in the snow. The Russians did not try to drive them back. Having rested, the boys got up and walked back across the sound to their positions on Vasikkasaari. Soon Mustasaari was again full of Russians.

Between four and five the artillery fire died down a little, just enough for the ear to sense the difference, but at five the concentration began to increase in severity. You could no longer gauge the power of the sound, it filled the whole world. At six the Russians drove ten tanks from the churchyard to the river bank. They crushed the gravestones in the cemetery and the few birches and mountain ash trees still standing there. Our men in the churchyard were surrounded. They were in a bad way. They had to come out of the churchyard on the run, with the Russians firing all their weapons at them. We lost many men there. One platoon was left in the churchyard. They must still be there.

When the Finns had already left the churchyard, the Russians attacked it from two directions, killing many of their own men and fighting each other on the crest of the hill. We could not enjoy the sight very much, although we could see it plainly. From the churchyard hill, the Russians had a clear sight line to fire direct-trajectory guns at our positions, and tanks were coming loudly clanking and banging toward the station. They began darting back and forth, taking aim at us and firing full blast.

I figured we wouldn't get much peace that evening, but the

Russian artillery ended their shift and shut down their war for the day. We began to gnaw on hardtack. We did not see any warm food that day, which is easy to understand. In the evening Battalion Commander Valtonen came to our positions with the company commander. He asked if we would be able to stand our ground. We figured that if nothing worse than Russian planes and artillery concentrations and tanks and infantry and mortar shells and machine guns came our way, we would not have to leave our positions. If anything worse came along, we could not guarantee it.

The battalion commander told us that Light Detachment 8, a cavalry squadron made up of men from Nurmo, had been assigned to aid us. They had rested for the entire Winter War, and had almost a full complement of men in good condition. With their aid, Matti Laurila planned to wipe the Russians out of the churchyard and take it over. It too easy for the Russians to fire over a large part of the Äyräpää ridge with their direct-trajectory guns.

"Stamp it approved," Laurila is reported to have said when he heard that the men from Nurmo were on their way to Äyräpää. They no longer had their mounts with them. Horses would only have been in the way here, in open terrain, under fire from automatic weapons. We knew Valtonen, the new battalion commander, well. He had been our battalion commander for a time at Terenttilä after Järvinen had frozen his foot while trying to drive the Russians from the Terenttilä swamp and the Mustaoja gully. Valtonen was of the opinion that we would be able to resist the neighbor's men since we'd had a chance to lie there for a day and watch the boys fighting.

XXIV

At night we heard the boys fighting on the islands. They had tried to take Mustasaari back from the Russians, but it was too late. During the evening and night, the Russians had brought in new troops and lots of military hardware. The boys were unable to take the island. We heard about it in the morning, and we saw it too.

The men from Nurmo attacked the churchyard hill at six o'clock. Their attack started off wrong to begin with. Daylight arrived and the artillery strike, which did no damage to the Russians, came too soon. The attack was like a cavalry charge without the horses. The intent was to charge the hill and take it by force from the Russians, but there were too few men for such an attack. Confronting them in the open terrain were so many automatic rifles and machine guns and direct-fire cannons brought there during the night that the Russians were firing nearly shoulder to shoulder. No one could run through that fire, and the men from Nurmo began dropping right at the start, killed and wounded. They were stopped long before they reached the hill, and they lay exposed to the Russian fire with no cover of any kind. In ten minutes, forty-two of them were dead and all the rest wounded, or almost all the rest. They realized they would not be attending service that day on the Äyräpää church hill, that another kind of congregation was going to church there. It was the morning of March fifth.

The Russians kept firing at the men from Nurmo the entire time they were trying to withdraw. They had no intention of letting them get back to their own lines. Such was the attack of Light Detachment 8 on the Äyräpää church hill. They did not get to church, nor back from their trip to the church. Their dead had to be left there — they got back only one body and their wounded.

The attempt of the men from Nurmo caused the Russians no trouble: they brushed it aside and went on about their other work. They had an attack of their own going on at the same time from Mustasaari to Vasikkasaari. But that was a better morning workout, and the Russians hadn't yet made it to Vasikkasaari. That happened only at about ten in the morning when they really started to attack with large forces and the support of all their weapons. Then they made it to the island. Nothing could stop them.

That day we weren't able to watch the others fighting for long. Our neighbor now began exerting pressure on our sector. He wanted badly to get to the river bank, and spared neither men nor materiel in the effort. Planes started to buzz over us and the artillery began a relentless fire on our positions. The infantry and tanks attacked before ten in the morning, but the boys set fire to two tanks in front of our positions. That slightly dampened the enthusiasm of the tank men. After ten, the infantry no longer came at us, but the artillery and the aerial bombs were on us all the time. We lost men to them. We piled the dead in back of our positions, and tried to bandage the wounded and take them to the river bank. The explosions and weapons fire and the screams of the wounded were deafening.

The Russians came from their position at the ferry landing, and the company next to us had to yield the ground from there to the church. The Russians already had the islands, and they quickly brought in a lot of military goods: tanks and automatic weapons and manpower as well. They had plenty of it. We were forced to leave our snow pits near the station and establish a line running from the ski jump along the edge of Kattilasuo, then turning sharply to the river bank. From long experience we knew that the Russians must never be left in peace in positions they had taken from us, but that we had to try driving them out before they had a chance to dig in. They always did so quickly and if a Russian once had time to dig in, it was hard to convince him that he had to leave.

We assembled a strike force to drive the Russians from the ferry landing. The first battalion, or what was still left of it, was brought up from the ferry landing to Kattilasuo. Our battalion was drawn up past the ski jump toward the river bank. We intended to hold these positions, but we had to try to drive the Russians from the river bank. From its brink they could fire almost unimpeded along the ice and over the river to the Vuosalmi side.

The boys from the first battalion went to roll up the Russian positions from the river bank and we went up the slope of the bank toward the church. Our neighbor had not had time to set up housekeeping yet. We came on the run into the positions where there was a confusion of men and units and tanks after their charge to the river bank. They were sorting things out there, but we didn't give them time to do it. We got the Russians cleaned out of the whole area from the ferry landing to the railway. We did not make it to the church hill; the resistance was too stiff there, and we began to lose boys to the machine-gun fire. So we had to draw back from the church hill and the edge of the cemetery to our own positions. Soon our neighbor came charging again and took possession of part of the shore. I remember that there were a lot of bodies at the foot of the church hill, Finnish and Russian boys mixed up, side by side and atop one another.

We were not able to hold the shore, for too many Russians kept coming and there was too much iron in the air for us. When the first battalion established its line, the church hill and the shoreline were in our neighbor's possession and the stretch from the railway line to the shore belonged to boys of the first battalion.

We set off along the ridge to our own positions, carrying our wounded and dead with us. The Russians were so confused by our attack that they did not start firing, and we were able to carry our boys in peace to our own side. We tried to take the wounded across the river to the Vuosalmi side for bandaging, but the Russians were firing at the ice from the church hill. Many of the wounded and their drivers and horses were lost in that fire. We could do nothing but leave the wounded lying on the Äyräpää side to suffer. The bodies which had been gathered from morning on were piled up to wait for the night transport. The wounded had to be left in the open air. We tried to find nooks for them in the river bank into which the Russians could not fire directly. The wounded lay there all day.

I was in position next to the ski jump. There the Russians did not try to come through. They had decided that the best place to cross was at the ferry, where the river was narrowest.

From there they could advance by way of the islands, so they concentrated the entire force of their attack on the ferry landing and the islands. They could not get through at the ferry landing because there we had control of both banks of the river. Advancing into our machine gun fire spelled trouble for them. In the evening, however, the Russians did try to cross from the ferry landing in force. They did not make it. We shot a lot of them with our machine guns. In the morning they lay there so thick it looked as if someone had tried to cover the ice with dead bodies — as if someone, somewhere had wished that not a patch of white be seen by the human eye on that part of the Vuoksi. The ice was literally black with Russian bodies. They had no snow uniforms, only long overcoats and pointed caps, but they all had good felt boots. That was one good thing they had.

So the Russians did not try to come into our positions, which we worked to improve. Then we began to look around to see how we would spend the night. There would be no replacements. Practically all the men were tied to the front lines, that is, all the men who were left of Laurila's regiment.

We waited for food. When there was no sign of it, the boys crossed the river in the darkness and returned with bread and cheese. There was a pressing need for something to drink. We went to shell holes in the ice of the Vuoksi, fetched water in our mess kits, and tried to heat it. It was kind of a mix-up, a little flickering flame and many mess kits set over and around it to heat. When we began to drink the water, the pieces of ice in it had not yet melted.

That entire night we again heard the sounds of vehicles being driven on the Russian side, but they did not come from opposite our positions; they came from farther on down the line. There was a lot of noise from the station area and the church hill. We figured the boys there would be in a grim fix tomorrow. We also wondered if the enemy would get through the lines in the morning, and how things would turn out if the Russians got between us and the river. We went to the riverbank during the night to see where we might cross if we were forced to.

XXXV

In the morning the boys went to the river again to get water in their mess kits with which to wash down their hardtack and cheese. We stayed in our positions to keep the tiny campfire alive. When the boys came back they told us that the Russians were pouring from the tip of Vasikkasaari onto the Vuosalmi side. There was no one there to stop them. The company commander went to find out what was up.

It looked to be a nice day. The sun rose into a clear blue sky. We knew the planes would soon be over us. I went to the bank of the river and looked over at the Vuosalmi side to see if any of our boys were putting up a fight there or if we had been isolated in Äyräpää. On his way back from battalion, the company commander ordered me back to our positions. He said we had not been forgotten. The first battalion was in its old position near the station and the third battalion held the ferry landings on both sides of the Vuoksi. The Russians would have a hard time crossing there.

The planes were over us now and the artillery concentration began, but they did not dump their iron on our positions. Instead it fell on the ferry landing and on the Liete meadows on the Vuosalmi side of the Vuoksi. Tanks were already moving about on the opposite shore. We took up our positions and had to lie there that day. The Russians did not attack us here, but fired just enough artillery rounds to remind us of their existence. They were fighting on the ferry landing and the Liete meadows.

The company commander said that Hersalo's regiment, which had been responsible for that sector of the front, had allowed the Russians to cross the river. Their panzer arm was now creating havoc in the Liete meadows. I blessed the place we were in, the Kattilasuo ski jumping hill. The Russians did not seem interested in it. The food situation and that fact that none of us had had a decent sleep for days were our worst miseries that day. We were all down in the dumps, with no sorrow to spare for the boys from other battalions.

At night we received an order to attack the Äyräpää church hill in the morning and take it from the Russians. It was grim news. We remembered what had happened to the men of Detachment 8 from Nurmo when they set off for church on the morning of the fifth. Very few had come back on their own two feet. They had been tossed in to be chopped up by Russian machine-gun and direct-trajectory artillery fire.

We had to attack at six in the morning so we spent the whole night getting our gear and weapons ready. This time the artillery was supposed to fire a decent strike on the church. We knew that the Russians were deeply dug in on the hill, since they had had two days to dig holes and firing stations. Hand grenades and rifle fire would not drive them out.

At about four in the morning the battalion commander came to the ski-jump hill to check that we had everything ready. He did not have much to say.

"We have to do this now," he told us.

We didn't argue with him. We could see he had no say in the

matter. Some replacements from the Hersalo regiment arrived, even though that outfit must have had its hands full trying to drive the Russians from the Liete meadows. We lay there waiting for our time on this earth to be up soon. Few of us, we felt, would come walking back from the Äyräpää church hill that morning. We wouldn't get to church that day.

The artillery strike was supposed to begin at five-thirty. We listened, but did not hear it. As we lay or stood about on the ski-jump grounds waiting for the order to move out, the battalion commander's messenger arrived with the news that the attack order had been rescinded. That meant there was something else for us to do; we guessed it from the sounds we heard from Vasikkasaari and the other side of the Vuoksi.

When I had first heard the news of the attack, I had gone almost limp. It was as if life had been drained from me. And I let it happen because there was nothing I could do about it. Now I felt as if my life had been given back to me, but at first I could do nothing with that life. Sleeplessness and hunger, having my life taken from me and given back to me — it all left me so weak I had to sit down on the mix of black snow, sand, and tree limbs and hold on to keep from crying.

We were taken back to our positions and began to prepare food or to heat water from the Vuoksi in our mess kits. A heavy battle was going on around us, at the ferry landing and on the Liete meadows and on Vasikkasaari, but they did not need us to fight that day. The Russians left us in peace all day long. Only their artillery and airplanes remembered us, and we lost a few boys to them, but their panzers and infantry were fighting to the left of the battalion and on the islands in the river.

Our artillery had enough strength now to keep firing on the tip of Vasikkasaari all day, penning the Russians on the island and preventing them from bringing more troops and equipment over the river to the Liete meadows. They had control of a small piece of land on the Vuosalmi side, but they could not advance beyond it, for Hersalo's men were beyond the Liete meadows blocking the way. No further troops could cross the river during the day to come to the aid of the Russians.

In the evening we were informed that on the following day, which was the eighth of March, units would be pieced together from the Laurila and Hersalo regiments to push the Russians back across the Vuoksi in the Vasikkasaari area and to take the three islands, Vasikkasaari, Mustasaari, and Dynamosaari, from our neighbor, thus easing the pressure on Vuosalmi.

The movement of troops across the river began at night. We tried to move silently, as men who fear death can; during the day the Russians had a direct view of the place where we were crossing. Their artillery men must surely remember its coordinates and be eager to fire. But they did not fire then. Often they did not fight at night, but only moved their troops, concentrating them at some point, and keeping their vehicle engines warm. So we got across the Vuoksi to the Vuosalmi side and were taken through the woods and over the roads to the terrain beyond the Liete meadows.

There were already quite a number of our troops there from both regiments, Laurila's and Hersalo's. A decision had been made to push the Russians back to the Äyräpää side of the Vuoksi once and for all. It had to be done if we wanted to stay in Vuosalmi. Everyone who could be spared from the lines was there: all the supply men, the drivers and messengers and cooks and the infantry troops, of course, and the engineers. We had been made into a special strike force, many companies of us.

Laurila came in the very early morning and told the men from Järvenkylä to attack first. Nearly a company of their engineers had survived intact. They had mined the ground out front and in the rear during the entire war, and had burned Karelian villages. They refused to go and attack the Liete meadows, for it was an open place and beyond it the Russians had tanks and machine guns to fire directly across the meadows. Their company commander told Laurila that he would not have his men killed for nothing, but that Laurila could have men from other parishes killed if he thought it was necessary. They say the company commander was a lieutenant, the son of a vicar.

Laurila did not force the Järvenkylä men to go. He felt that dying was something of a private matter, even though we were in a war. For that reason he was known among line officers as a leader who tried to spare the men from Ostrobothnia, since he himself was from there and knew the men well. He did not force the Järvenkylä men to go; he believed that among the men of Ostrobothnia a number could be found who were willing to give up their lives for their country.

Laurila then told the company commander of the men from Peräseinäjoki, a Lieutenant Kirkkala, that his men were to take the lead and hurl the Russians onto the Vuoksi, that the others would follow and drive them to the Äyräpää side. Kirkkala did not say a word. He was wearing a cap with an impossibly long visor on it, a mere summer cap. He pulled the visor down over his face and left without saying a word.

Day began to dawn. The artillery opened fire at six while we lay in the woods in back of the Liete meadows. We could see our own artillery scoring hits on the Russian bridgehead positions and on the tip of Vasikkasaari. The men from Peräseinäjoki launched their attack on the meadows with their company commander in the lead. We could see that few of the boys from Peräseinäjoki would come back intact. The lieutenant was hit after he had run fifty meters into the open from the edge of the woods. Men fell behind and to either side of him and began shouting for the medics. Some of the men from Peräseinäjoki kept on running, with the Russians firing on them from their positions the entire time.

The rest of us rose from the roots of trees and stumps to join the attack. We ran shouting toward the river bank.

For some reason the Russians were seized by a fear that we would overrun them. They rose from their safe holes and started on a jaunt across the ice. That was a mistake. We shot them as they rose from the holes and ran down the bank. On the river, they were mowed down by the artillery and all the infantry weapons.

The din and shouting and the banging of weapons was huge. The battle became an awful slaughter, for the Russians had panicked. In a panic one can't think clearly. He tries to run faster than a bullet, but he can't. The bullet catches him, or the artillery shell, and he dies on the spot. That's exactly what happened to the Russians. They were in good positions at the edge of the Liete meadows, but they were frightened by our artillery concentration. They were not used to artillery fire. The attack by the men from Peräseinäjoki and the rest of us caused them to panic and run across the river to Vasikkasaari. There our artillery hammered them with all its guns, and, as we learned later, with the last of its shells. No living person could last long there, he either got out or died.

XXXVI

When we got across the Liete meadows and into the positions abandoned by the Russians, they were already running on Vasikkasaari. Many had thrown their weapons away. Some had even tossed their overcoats onto the ice and the shore of the island to get through the snow faster. None of them ran faster than the bullets or the shells, though.

Running over the Liete meadows had tired us all so much that we remained lying on the river bank. A command came down immediately that we could not lie there but had to push on over the sound and take the islands now that the enemy had abandoned them. Our artillery fire shifted from the islands to the Äyräpää church shore, where the Russians were now running up the slope toward their homeland.

We rose and ran down the slope and onto the ice of the river, which was dotted with holes chopped by the artillery. We ran, dodging the holes and leaping over the wounded and dead bodies of Russians. We ran through the broken and frozen reeds, which crackled as they fell. We reached the shore of Vasikkasaari, but now the crackling was that of Russian machine guns and artillery firing on us from the ridges on the Äyräpää side.

Vasikkasaari had been ground into a black shambles by

artillery fire. We could not go beyond it; our strength simply gave out. Although the officers and non-coms tried to get us to go on to Mustasaari and Dynamosaari, we just lay in the shell holes and the positions that our men and the Russians had once dug there, while the Russians showered iron down on us again.

We could not go anywhere, we had to lie there on Vasikkasaari that day. Only when twilight fell did we draw back to the Vuosalmi side — those of us who could, who were still alive. As we lay under Russian fire during the day, a lieutenant from the Hersalo regiment shot a wounded Russian with his pistol. He could not stand the screams of the wounded man, and shot him in the forehead like a ram. We didn't like it at all, even though we'd seen all kinds of brutality. But we'd never seen a man shot like that.

At night, after we had left, the Russians took back Vasikkasaari. They did not, however, make it to the Vuosalmi side even on the following day. They did try to drive us from the river bank near the Liete meadows, but the men of Hersalo's regiment would not let them cross the river.

We were able to spend the next day in our positions near the ski-jump hill, where we were better off. Only the Russian artillery and the air arm lashed at us there. The Russians attacked and tried to cross the river to the Liete meadows, but the boys stopped them. They stopped the Russians even though they were driven into the Finnish artillery and machine gun fire in such a way that I thought somewhere a dam had been opened before a huge flood, and that the flood would roll irresistibly over everything below it. The Russians just would not believe they could not cross the Vuoksi at that point.

Nevertheless on the afternoon of the tenth they did get across to the Vuosalmi side from Vasikkasaari, and the Hersalo men had to move their line to the edge of the woods beyond the Liete meadows. Again the Russians quickly brought a lot of military equipment across the river, although our artillery tried to fire on Vasikkasaari. The Russian tanks drove around the Liete meadows firing at everything they saw, at trees, bushes, and the men among them. All the while the Russian direct-trajectory guns were also firing, but when their infantry tried to cross the Liete meadows, our men would not let them.

Hersalo's men fought there for two days, the eleventh and twelfth of March. Laurila's men fought at the ferry landings on both sides of the river. The Russians did not get through, although they badly wanted to and did not spare their men.

Now the Russians no longer tried to break into our sector in large numbers. We had to fear and freeze and go hungry while artillery hacked at us and fighter planes strafed us and bombers dumped their loads on us. But no large infantry units tried to drive us from the ski-jump hill at Kattilasuo, although smaller detachments did have a go at our positions. We lost many wounded on both days. It was on the morning of the eleventh that I woke up in my snow pit with my head frozen to the ground and got the lifelong headache.

On the thirteenth of March the Russians began a heavy artillery concentration. We lay in the pits we had tried to dig, in bomb craters, and in deep holes dug into the frozen ground by the heavy artillery. All those holes seemed shallow in that concentration of fire. The Russians fired with all their weapons for five hours. At about eleven the artillery fire ceased and there was complete silence. The battalion commander's messenger arrived and told us that peace had been made between Finland and Russia. We hadn't gotten word of it earlier because of the artillery concentration.

We tried to peer out and see what the word "peace" meant to the Russians. Everything was so silent that our ears hurt. We saw that the Russians were also peering at us from their holes; they were only fifty meters away. The Russians began to rise up to the banks of their firing pits, signaling and waving their hands at us. They did not dare to come out of their holes, nor did we. We did not exactly trust that peace agreement. We watched for a quarter of an hour to see if our neighbor would start shooting or otherwise raining metal from the sky. Then the Russians got out of their holes and started walking over to our side. They were shouting something, "Mir, mir...." It means "Peace." They had no weapons in their hands, but there were many of them, many hundreds. There were only eight of us boys, and we got up out of our pits and walked out toward the Russian positions through the trees which had been mowed down by artillery fire. The Russians felt our arms and the flesh or our cheeks and babbled something to each other which we did not understand. We were an awful sight, so thin and bearded and dirty that it was hard to recognize us as human beings.

Our neighbors began showing us photographs of Russian people, of men and women and children, and offered us cigarettes. We had nothing to offer them. We had not dared to leave our weapons in our positions. The Russians pointed to them and said something and made a face, then showed us their empty hands and began hugging us.

Soon their officers ordered them back to their positions and we went to sit in our pits. Officers came from the Russian side and we saw Matti Laurila and some of our officers walk to meet them between the lines. We heard later that they had made an agreement about the manner in which the Finnish soldiers were to leave their positions and head for home. Matti Laurila had asked that we be allowed to take away the bodies of the men from Nurmo who were lying in the Äyräpää churchyard in full view of us, along with the bodies of our other boys, but the Russians would not agree to it. They did say that they would arrange a military burial for them. I sat at the bottom of a pit, planning to wait for the next order. I could not bring myself to do anything. When the company commander came, we asked him what direction we would take now. He got angry and shouted that of course we would head for the old border, perhaps for Metsäpirtti or Rautu. He had the idea that we had won the war. Everybody thought so.

We were bitter when we heard the peace terms that afternoon. And we were bitter when we had to march for three days from *The Isthmus* toward our homeland before we arrived at the new border.